Waking Up Married

Mira Lyn Kelly

First published in Great Britain 2013
by Mills & Boon, an imprint of Harlequin (UK) Limited.
Harlequin (UK) Limited, Eton House, 18-24 Paradise Road,
Richmond, Surrey TW9 1SR

© Mira Lyn Sperl 2012

ISBN: 978 0 263 23454 1

Harlequin (UK) policy is to use papers that are natural, renewable and recyclable products and made from wood grown in sustainable forests. The logging and manufacturing process conform to the legal environmental regulations of the country of origin.

Printed and bound in Great Britain
by CPI Antony Rowe, Chippenham, Wiltshire

About Mira Lyn Kelly

Mira Lyn Kelly grew up in the Chicago area and earned her degree in fine arts from Loyola University. She met the love of her life while studying abroad in Rome, Italy, only to discover he'd been living right around the corner from her for the previous two years. Having spent her twenties working and playing in the Windy City, she's now settled with her husband in rural Minnesota, where their four beautiful children provide an excess of action, adventure and entertainment.

With writing as her passion, and inspiration striking at the most unpredictable times, Mira can always be found with a notebook at the ready. (More than once the neighbours have caught her, covered in grass clippings, scribbling away atop the compost container!)

When she isn't reading, writing or running to keep up with the kids, she loves watching movies, blabbing with the girls and cooking with her husband and friends. Check out her website, **www.miralynkelly.com**, for the latest dish!

Also by Mira Lyn Kelly

Wild Fling or a Wedding Ring?
Front Page Affair
The S Before Ex
Tabloid Affair, Secretly Pregnant!

Did you know these are also available as eBooks?
Visit www.millsandboon.co.uk

TM

This book is dedicated with love to my dad,
for always supporting my dreams—
no matter where they took me!
(Okay, that's far enough, Dad. No reading past here!)

CHAPTER ONE

FORCED TO LISTEN to one heaving revolt after another reverberate off the polished marble, Connor Reed cursed his conscience.

Talk about an inconvenient burden. No matter how his stomach rocked and his head slammed, there was no way he could make a bolt for the beckoning doorway to freedom at the far wall.

Wrenching his gaze back to his own slightly green reflection, he turned off the tap and wrung out a towel. Pushed some empathy into his expression and prepared to face the music.

"Hey, gorgeous," he called, crossing over to the pitiful creature half leaning into, half clutching the toilet in front of her. "Feeling any better?"

Raccoon eyes peered out from beneath a blond rat's nest as she reached for the damp cloth he held in offering. "Carter—"

"Connor," he corrected drily, torn between amusement and what, by all rights, ought to be the very antithesis of it.

"We need a lawyer," she gasped, barely finding the time to look chagrined before the next wave of revolt took her.

A lawyer. Not exactly a stellar kickoff to their honeymoon. But then, this wasn't exactly a stellar situation to begin with. Of course, in the less than fifteen minutes since the warm body sprawled beside him had moaned—once, and not in a good way—then lurched from the bed to the bathroom, he hadn't quite put all the soggy pieces of the night before into place. But based on the shocking evidence at hand—or more specifically, finger...and the band of glinting diamonds encircling hers—this was the worst-case scenario come to life. Cutting loose gone bad. Consequences in action. Yeah, in all likelihood, this was going to be a major hassle to clean up.

So a lawyer sounded like an ideal place to start. Once the upchuck portion of the morning concluded, at any rate.

"One thing at a time, babe. Let's get through this, and we'll worry about the rest later."

Whatever her choked response was, he got the gist it was an agreement of sorts.

Damn, what a disaster.

Rubbing a hand over the back of his neck, Connor gave his blanching bride a not-so-subtle once-over.

Twelve hours ago she'd been "authentic" with her sharp wit and gently rough edges. Her too-wide smile, assortment of freckles and sexy laugh. Now, with her hair threatening to dip into God only knew, she just looked…rough. No gentle about it.

Still, even as he stared at the hot mess she was before him, fragmented images bombarded his mind with hints of who she'd been the night before. The girl-next-door giving in to a bit of wild. The perfect fit for his bad-boy mood. He'd thought she looked like a few hours of fun.

So how the hell had she ended up flipped over his shoulder, giggling about how crazy he was, as he toted her into one of those all-night chapels Las Vegas was famous for?

Megan turned, giving him a full-on frontal view of the too-tight, hot-pink T-shirt she'd been wearing when he'd stumbled into the bathroom after her.

Stamped across her bust in black block letters were two words: *GOT SPERM?*

Oh, right. That was how.

Hell.

What had she been thinking!

Megan peered up at the darkening scowl across Carter's—no—*Connor's* face and then down at what was probably a combined ten carats of diamonds adorning the fourth finger of her left hand…and heaved into the bowl again.

She'd had sex. With a stranger. Someone she maintained only the foggiest recollection of meeting. And then…she'd gone and *married* him.

Or maybe they'd waited…going the more traditional route and saving themselves for after the wedding. So it would be special.

Ugh!

So *incredibly special* the only detail of the entire consummation she remembered was the soft rub of fabric between her thighs, the heady weight of him above her and her intense frustration in getting her toe caught in his belt loop while trying to wrestle his tie loose.

And now, here she was on her knees, hurling her lungs out while this man, essentially a stranger, bore witness to one of the most intimate unpleasantnesses a person could endure. She wished he'd left when she'd told him to. But he'd stayed to make sure she was okay…like the good husband he was.

It was almost enough to make her laugh, only it really wasn't funny and her body was otherwise engaged.

"There can't be much left" came the gruff voice from behind her.

As the spasms subsided, she hazarded a glance at the man she'd married. Beyond the contemplative expression, those dark eyes didn't offer up much to read.

"There isn't…" she groaned. "I've been on empty for a few rounds already. This…is just my stomach making a point…I think."

"Hmm. Really driving it home, I see." The touch of dry humor pulled her focus back to him again. To the details she'd missed in the first pass. He was tall. And not because of her near-floor-level perspective. Tall enough so as he leaned against the open doorway, his free hand hung in a loose grip from the top of the frame mere inches from his head. And he was built in a powerful, lean-strength kind of way where the muscles across his chest, abdomen, shoulders and arms were well-defined but without the extreme bulk of serious bodybuilders. This guy just looked really fit. And as if that weren't bad enough, he was classically handsome too, with a blade-straight nose, high cheekbones and an assortment of even features so appealing she suddenly wondered how long she'd been staring.

From her little hangout on the floor...by the toilet...where she'd been throwing up.

Ugh!

Really, the humiliation couldn't get much worse. But it didn't matter. This guy and all his good looks weren't a part of her plan. So what if he was handsome, or that she'd seen hints of the kind of humor she typically appreciated, or that she was, in fact, married to him? She'd had enough close calls in her life with men she'd actually *known*, and she was through with the whole business.

Still, pride had her stumbling to her feet on limbs that were clumsy and tight from the combination of dehydration and kneeling too long. Limbs that weren't quite working. Suddenly she was going right back down until two strong hands gripped her beneath her arms, holding her steady as she regained her footing.

The contact was awkward. Her, trying to hold herself apart; him, trying to support her without getting too close. "Thank you."

"Not a problem." And then after a pause, "Just one of the benefits of having a husband around, I guess."

She nodded, exhausted, overwhelmed, but somehow more grateful than words could convey for that bit of superficial exchange. As much as they needed to, she wasn't ready to talk about what happened last night. About how they were going to sort it out this morning and over the next however long it took to get an annulment processed.

Not until she'd at the very least had a shower, tooth-brushing, floss and several intensive minutes with the most mediciney mouthwash she could get her hands on. Glancing down, she added a change of clothes to her list. And then, committed to doing her part, she replied in kind, "Knew there was a reason I'd picked one up."

The low answering chuckle had her daring another look over her shoulder.

It was the smile that did it. That brought the melee of vodka-soaked images into order enough for her to see at least a glimpse of the man from the night before rather than the near stranger she'd woken beside this morning.

Oh, God. What had she gotten herself into—and how fast could she get herself out of it?

CHAPTER TWO

Twelve hours earlier...

"OH, COME ON, screw the sperm bank." Tina sighed with a dismissive flutter of her candy-apple acrylics. "Where's the fun in that?"

Megan Scott tipped her glass, swallowing the last decadent drops of white-chocolate martini, then slumped deeper into the plush cushions of the lounge chair she'd taken up residence in some forty minutes before. Contemplating another drink, she did her best to ignore the incessant bickering her fellow bridesmaids had perfected through a lifetime of practice.

That it was her womb they were battling over was of as little consequence as the fact that Megan already had a plan and she was sticking to it.

"Um...the fun comes nine months later," Jodie snipped back. "All tiny and new, wearing one of those little nursery beanies... and without any of the communicable side effects on offer with *your* plan..."

Tina's plan, as Megan understood it, revolved around the T-shirt—hot off the silk screen and sporting the slogan GOT SPERM?—folded neatly on the cocktail table between them.

"I mean, seriously, who's to say this total, random stranger enticed by your thirteen-dollar custom call for baby batter isn't attempting to walk off the early stages of Ebola or worse? Casual, unprotected sex is stupid. And you're trying to talk Megan into it. For God sake, why don't you pick up a knife and stab her."

Turning the glass upside down, Megan watched as a single last drop of martini goodness slid to the rim. Catching it with her tongue, she hoped the cocktail waitress would take her action as the plea for help it was and bring a refill. Fast.

"You're such a prude. It's pathetic."

Eesh.

"*What I am* is too much of a lady to say *what you are.*"

"Girls, please," Megan interjected before the volley of barbs got any more intense. "I totally appreciate you two looking out for me this way." Okay, she was stretching the truth, but somehow her tongue let her get away with it. Honestly, she'd have rather been of such little interest they both got her name wrong all weekend and ignored her through dinner. But courtesy of her mother's propensity to spill secrets, the family grapevine had guaranteed her Vegas arrival for cousin Gail's wedding was met with a tempest of polarizing opinion regarding her decision to undergo artificial insemination in two months' time. "Tina, I love—really love—this T-shirt, but the only place it's going is into my scrapbook. And, Jodie, thank you for the support but—"

Jodie's hand came up, cutting her off. "I don't, really. Support what you've decided to do. You ought to wait to find a husband like the rest of us."

Images of Barry and the two years they'd dated flashed through her mind, threatening to suck her into a vortex of churning emotions she wouldn't allow herself to surrender to. Shame, embarrassment, anger and helpless frustration.

"Megan, I swear I didn't even realize it myself. Not until right that minute…and suddenly I knew. I'd never stopped loving her."

She wasn't going there again, wasn't wasting another precious second on the man who'd left for a conference talking about starting a family with her and then come home married to someone else.

Spine stiffening, she reined herself in.

She didn't need Barry.

She didn't need any man to have the child she'd always wanted—well, at least not for more than five minutes of quality time with a plastic cup.

Jodie sighed, a faraway look settling over her features. "Wait for your Prince Charming and you'll have someone to share your special moment in the nursery, making it all the sweeter."

"Well, actually," Megan started, but Jodie wasn't finished.

"You're what's wrong with our society. I mean, life isn't about getting everything you want the instant you want it. Some things are worth waiting for. That said, in a toss-up between bedding down with the next patient zero or hitting the drive-thru for prescreened sperm…I'll back the bank."

Megan felt the telling wash of heat rush through her cheeks, but thinking about Gail and what kind of wedding she'd have if all three of her bridesmaids were at each other's throats, she tamped it down. "Okay. Well, thank you…for your thoughts on the issue."

Tina's less-than-delicate snort sounded from beside her, and Megan craned her neck in search of their waitress. Only, rather than the leggy server with the no-nonsense attitude, she found her attention snared by the man walking past their table. Hand raised in casual greeting, mahogany eyes fixed on someone across the room, he was tall, dark and handsome in the most traditional sense. Broad and tapered, chiseled and cut. All clean lines and classic good looks. The balanced symmetry of him so flawless, it might have made him bland.

If not for his mouth.

This guy had one of those slanted smiles going on. The kind so lazy only half of it bothered to go to work. And yet, something about the ease of it suggested a near permanence on his face, while its stunted progress implied—well, she supposed that was part of the lure. It could really imply anything.

That smile was the kind women got lost in while trying to unravel its mystery.

Only, Megan was through trying to read signs and figure guys out. Which was why she pried her eyes loose from the table where this one had settled in with a friend or associate or

whomever, and forced herself to refocus on Tina and Jodie…
who were totally focused on her.

In tandem they leaned forward, resting on their elbows.

"Window-shopping the gene pool, Megan?" Tina asked with
a knowing smirk as one pencil-thin brow pushed high. "See
something you like?"

Jodie's eyes narrowed. "His suit is too perfectly cut to be anything but made-to-measure. The suit, the watch, the links. This
guy has *quality catch* written all over him. Megan, quick, cross
your legs higher and give up some thigh. Tina, get his attention."

Megan's lips parted to protest, but Tina was a woman of action. "Wow, Megan, I knew you were a gymnast, but I didn't
think anyone's legs could do that!"

Tina's face took on an expression of benevolence and she
crossed her arms, leaning back in her seat. "You're welcome."

Needles of tension prickled up and down her back as she
struggled for her next breath. Eyes fixed on the tabletop in front
of her, Megan held up her empty martini glass and prayed to the
cocktail gods for a refill. When she thought she could manage
more than a squeak, she cleared her throat and replied to anyone within listening distance, "I'm not a gymnast."

At which point Tina and Jodie burst out laughing.

"It may not seem like it now, but you're better off without her…"

Connor Reed shifted irritably in his chair, swirling the amber
and ice of his scotch as he listened to Jeff Norton forfeit his status as one of the guys. "Noted."

And not exactly a news flash.

"…You and Caro were together for almost a year… It's okay
to be hurt…"

Hurt? Connor's eye started to twitch.

This wasn't guy talk. It wasn't the promised blowing off of
steam with which he'd been lured to Sin City.

It *wasn't* cool.

"…a blow to the ego, and for someone with an ego like
yours…"

Growling into his glass, he muttered, "We need to get your testosterone levels checked."

"Whatever," Jeff answered, unfazed. He was as secure with his emotional "awareness" as he was with his position as Connor's oldest and best friend. "All I'm saying is you were ready to marry Caro two weeks ago. I don't believe you're as indifferent as you make out to be."

"Yeah, but you never want to believe the truth about me," Connor replied with an unrepentant grin. "Seriously, though, Jeff, like I told you before, I'm fine. Caro was a great girl, but hearing what she had to say...I'm more relieved than anything else."

The following grunt suggested Jeff wasn't buying it.

And to an extent, the guy might be right. Just not the way he figured.

Connor wasn't heartbroken over the end of the relationship because his heart had never played into the equation. Callous but true. And something Caro had understood from the first.

Connor didn't do love. All too well he understood the potential of its destructive power. He knew the distance of its reach, had experienced the devastation of its ripple effect. No thank you. He hadn't been signing on for more.

What he'd been after was a family. The kind he'd only ever seen from the outside looking in, but coveted just the same. The kind his father hadn't wanted some bastard son to contaminate, and his mother had been too deep in her own grief to sustain. So he'd been determined to build his own.

There were a lot of things he'd done without as a kid. Things he'd made it his purpose to secure as an adult. Money, respect, his own home...and the thriving business he ran with an iron fist that garnered them all. But a family...? For that, he needed a partner. One he'd thought he found in Caro. She fit the bill, fundraiser ready with the right name, education and background. Coolly composed and devoid of the emotional neediness he'd spent his adult life actively avoiding. Or so he'd thought, right up to that last day when she'd folded her napkin at the side of her plate and evenly explained she wanted a marriage based on more than what they had. She hadn't expected to, but there it was.

Fair enough. He gave her credit for having the good sense to recognize she wanted something she wouldn't find with him. And most important, *before* the vows were exchanged.

So, heartbroken? No.

Disappointed? Sure.

Relieved? Hell, yes.

"…I think you're lonely. Sad…"

Throwing back the rest of his single malt, Connor relished the burn down his throat and spread of heat through his belly. If he weighed in fifty pounds lighter, it might have been enough to fuzz out the discomfort of this conversation.

But there was always the next one.

"…remember, there are other fish in the sea—"

"*Come on*, what's next—hot flashes?" Holding up the empty, he scanned the crowd for the cocktail server.

"—hell, apparently the one over there is a gymnast."

Connor quirked a brow, angling his head for a better look. "Which one?"

Jeff winked. "Just making sure you were listening. Care about you, man."

Though he'd never figured out why, Connor knew.

That caring had been the single constant in his life from the time he'd been ripped out of poverty and drop-kicked into the East Coast's most exclusive boarding school at thirteen. He'd been the illegitimate kid with a chip on his shoulder, a jagged crack through the center of his soul and a grudge against the name he couldn't escape—and Jeff had been the unlucky SOB saddled with him as a roommate. Connor hadn't given him any reason to cut him a break, but for some reason, Jeff had anyway.

Which was why, for as much as he gave his friend a hard time about being an "in touch" guy…he also gave him the truth. "Yeah, you too… Now, where's the gymnast?"

Another two rounds and some forty minutes later, Connor leaned back in his chair watching as Jeff reasserted his status as a testosterone-driven male by smoothly intercepting the cocktail girl he'd been eyeing for the better part of an hour. Connor didn't even want to think about the rap this guy had laid on her to get those lashes batting and her tray cast aside so fast, but whatever it was, it must have been phenomenal.

Jeff shot him a salute, and the deal was done.

Reaching into this breast pocket, Connor pulled out his wallet, tossed a few bills onto the table and then set his empty glass atop the stack.

The night stretched out before him with all its endless... exhausting possibilities.

He could hit the blackjack tables.

Grab a bite.

Pick up some company. Or not. With this apathetic indifference he was rocking—

"Excuse me."

Glancing up, he'd expected another waitress ready to clear, but instead it was the blonde in the midnight dress from the other table. The *gymnast*, who most definitely wasn't a gymnast if her height and the soft S-like lines of a figure draped in one of those clingy wrap numbers were anything to go on.

Very nice. "Hi. What can I do for you?"

Her smile spread wide as her big blue eyes held his. "This is going to sound like a line. A really, really bad one. But you've got to believe me when I say it's not."

The corner of his mouth twitched as he readied for what inevitably was *the rest of the line*. Playing in, he gave her a nod. "Okay, you've got the disclaimer out of the way. Go for it."

She nodded, releasing a deep breath. "I noticed you were about to leave. And I'd be more grateful than you could imagine if you wouldn't mind walking out with me. So it looks like we're leaving *together*."

Right. "Just *looks* like we're leaving together?"

Again her wide smile flashed, and Connor saw shades of girl-next-door. Not usually his type, but for whatever reason, there was something about the look of this one...

"Yes. My...friends saw me notice you earlier and...well...

and you don't even want to know what it's been like since. I told them I'd come over and see if you were interested because I want them off my back. But I can tell from looking at you, that I'm not the kind of woman you'd be interested in...which is, actually, the only reason I decided to come over. I'd love to get out of here without them following me for the rest of the night."

She'd been checking him out, eh?

Well, fair being fair, he gave his eyes the go-ahead to run the length of her and back, spending more time along the way than he'd done in his first casual glance. Very, very nice. Even with her scolding finger wagging at him on the return trip.

"None of that. You're handsome, but I'm honestly working an escape strategy here."

He shifted, the smile he hadn't quite let loose earlier breaking free with the realization she was serious. Glancing past her, he noted her friends blatantly staring back.

"Subtle."

She shrugged delicately. "So far as I can tell, subtle isn't really their thing."

He raised a brow. "*So far as you can tell?* What kind of friends are they?"

"The kind on loan until our bridesmaids' obligations have been fulfilled, sometime before dawn on Sunday. I hope. They're my cousin's best friends from kindergarten."

Ah. "And they've taken an interest in your love life because....?"

Her nose wrinkled up as she scanned the ceiling. "Any chance you might just walk me out of here?"

Connor eased back into his chair, pulling out the seat Jeff had vacated with his foot. "Not if you want it to look convincing. I'll walk you out of here...in ten minutes."

The skeptical look said she'd figured out he was thinking about more than the next ten minutes.

As different as she was from the women he usually pursued, she looked as if she really might be exactly the kind of fun this night called for.

The kind who didn't generally hook up with strangers.

The corruptible kind, he thought, feeling less apathetic by the second.

"Ten minutes. We'll talk. Flirt. You can touch my arm once or twice to really sell it. Maybe I'll tuck some wayward strand of hair behind your ear. Your voyeuristic friends will gobble it up. Then I'll lean in close to your ear and suggest we get out of here. Maybe do it in a way that has you blushing all the way to your roots. You'll get flustered and shy, but let me take your hand anyway. And we'll go."

The look on her face was priceless. As though he'd gotten to her with this bit of scripted tripe.

"That's…um…" She swallowed, her gaze darting around, landing on his mouth and lingering briefly before snapping back to his eyes. "More of an investment than I was really asking for."

"The better for you."

"Yeah, but what's in it for you?"

Connor flashed a wolfish smile. "Ten minutes to convince you to give me twenty. We'll see where it goes from there."

The slight shake of her head had his focus honing and his critical skills tuning up. Man, he'd been thinking how much he might like to see her girl-next-door smile turn sultry, but now here she was making him work for her too? It didn't get better.

"I should probably go. I'm not a casual-encounter kind of girl. And even if you were looking for something more than casual, I still wouldn't be interested."

Something about the way she said it had his curiosity standing up for a stretch. "Oh, yeah—how come?"

Her hand lifted in a sort of dismissive flutter, which stopped almost before it began. Then meeting his eyes, she said, "Sorry, it's a little too personal for a *fake first nondate*."

Connor grinned, shrugging one shoulder. "So why not make it a *not-quite-so-fake first nondate*. Or maybe a *fake first date*, though if we're already faking it, we ought to go for a second or third date…when all the good stuff starts."

Her smile went wide before giving way to a laugh out of line with the girl-next-door everything else about her. The laugh had his head cranking around for a second take. And sure enough, when her eyes were half closed, her lips parted for that low rolling sound of seductive abandon, he was the one left staring.

For a second.

Before he shifted back into gear. "Seriously, I'd like to know."

He could see it in her eyes, in the tilt of her head and the way her body had already started to turn away. In her mind, the decision was made, and mentally, she was halfway to the door. Too bad.

But regardless, he didn't want to leave her hanging after she'd mustered the nerve to come over.

"I'll walk you out," he said, but she shook her head and smiled.

"Thanks, I'll be fine, though."

"Fair enough. I'm Connor, by the way." He extended his hand, feeling like an ass offering to shake goodbye after the exchange they'd shared, but for some reason wanting to test the contact anyway.

"Megan." She reached across the table and met his hand with her smaller one—and a flash of neon pink arced through the air, coming to land in his lap.

The hand in his clenched as he looked down and read the block lettering.

"What the—?"

Peals of laughter rang from the table where Megan had been sitting. The bridesmaids she'd been trying to escape. Or so she'd said.

His hand tightened around hers as, leveling her with a stare, he pulled her forward and then down into the open chair. "Sit. Now I *need* to know."

Megan looked into his eyes, a thousand thoughts running through hers before she slumped back in the chair and said, "Okay, Carter—"

"Connor."

She swallowed. "Connor. Right. Sorry. So here it is…"

CHAPTER THREE

Nine hours earlier...

"I THINK YOUR SUBCONSCIOUS is trying to tell you something."

Megan grinned into her glass, trying not to laugh as she took the next sip. Sweet martini goodness coated her tongue, making her wonder how she'd gone through so much of her life without having tried one of these white-chocolate concoctions. They were delicious.

Oh, wait…the subconscious…

"Okay, what?"

"This trip to Vegas. It's your subconscious screaming some deeply repressed need to take a chance. Do something crazy."

They were back to this again. Megan shot him a knowing look, only to find his unrepentant one on the other end. "*Or*, this trip is about my cousin getting married."

"Denial is a powerful thing."

"Forget it. I told you already. I'm not running off and marrying you, so please stop begging."

Carter—shoot, *Connor*, why couldn't she remember!—let out a bark of laughter. They both knew marriage wasn't what he'd been getting at. Just as they both knew he wasn't actually serious.

He knew what her plans were. Had been truly interested when she'd laid them out, explaining her choice to pursue artificial insemination via sperm donor. And rather than back away slowly, he'd decided they both needed a night to cut loose and have some fun. The kind without consequences. The kind that revolved around easy conversation, harmless flirting and more drinks than were a good idea.

Knowing it would be the last, and finding a certain comfort in the utter lack of expectation from the man she was with, Megan agreed.

And she'd been near breathless with laughter ever since—milling through the grand casino, stopping at one attraction and then another, caught up in the sort of fun in which she never indulged.

Connor had been right. This was what she'd needed.

The palm of his hand settled lightly at the small of her back as he guided her toward an outcropping of slots. "I don't know, Megan. Seems for a decision this big, you want to consider every option before dismissing it out of hand."

"Maybe you're right." Then giving in to the impish grin tugging at her lips, she waved vaguely at the men around her. "And there are plenty of *options* to consider."

Connor shook his head. "If you're looking for a guy to close the deal, I'd steer clear of the slots," he offered, totally deadpan. "Nothing says *compensation issues* like a man clinging too closely to a twelve-inch rod of metal."

It took more than she'd thought she had to do it, but once Megan reined in her laughter, she pulled a mock scowl. "Seriously, how long have we known each other—and you think I'd hit the slots?"

This time it was Connor cracking the half smile that seemed his equivalent to a full-on belly laugh. "Right, I should have had more faith."

She nodded, scanning the casino floor. "Roulette tables are where all the quality swimmers hang out."

Another wry twist of lips. "I'm forced to disagree with you. Any guy lingering around a game based solely on luck is delusional. Probably believes in Santa and fairies. Doesn't bode well for mental stability. You want the probability of psychosis spiraling through Junioretta's double helix?"

Another stifled giggle. "No, definitely not. How could I have been so off base?"

"Sometimes I wonder about you."

She couldn't remember the last time she'd had so much fun. Couldn't remember a guy she'd been so instantly at ease with. Of course, that last bit probably had more to do with knowing this wasn't leading anywhere. Which took the pressure off tremendously. She could simply enjoy the attention of this incredibly attractive, charming man without worrying about... anything.

"Blackjack, then?"

They'd made it halfway across the floor when Connor caught a passing waitress, giving her their order before returning his attention to Megan. "Also delusional. He thinks he's in control when it's a game of chance. Unless he's counting...and then you have a criminal element to consider."

Playing devil's advocate, she asked, "But wouldn't counting suggest a higher level of intelligence?"

"So you're a single mom, strapped from the cost of the private academy his 'genius' demands. How much time are you going to have for all those trips to visit little Buster in juvie?"

Megan let out her best indignant cough. "You're implying my baby is going to be some kind of delinquent?"

One oh-so-arrogant brow shot high. Sexy and confident. "Not if you play your cards right."

"Fine, fine." She laughed, wiping the tears at the corners of her eyes with the backs of her thumbs. "So we've been through the slots, roulette and blackjack. If none of those are right, then what—offtrack betting?"

Connor drew to a stop, turning to consider her more closely than the question called for. Closely enough she could feel her body respond to the touch of his eyes at every point of contact. His smile was pure arrogance as he answered, "You want to win the genetic jackpot, then skip the pit stop at Gamblers Anonymous altogether. Obviously your best bet is me."

* * *

Megan laughed, head thrown back, eyes closed, and the sound of it hit him right in the center of the chest. And when those big blue eyes blinked back at him, her cheeks a rosy red, the hot rush and warm pull of attraction firing through his body nearly knocked the reason right out of him.

Fortunately, she didn't seem to notice as she turned to accept her cocktail from the approaching waitress. "In the nick of time. I'll definitely need another drink before I buy into that one."

With a jut of his chin, he urged, "By all means, then, bottoms up." Tossing back a swallow of his own, he grinned. "I've got all night."

Damn, she had a gorgeous laugh. Even after it left her lips… echoes of it lit her eyes. Those sparkling eyes that were staring up at him like maybe he had the solution for anything. And suddenly, the idea of this strong, fiercely independent woman *needing* something *from him* appealed on an almost primal level.

"What?" he asked, chalking up the low timbre of his voice to a dry throat and remedying the obvious problem with a gulp of scotch.

Megan reached for the lapel of his jacket, her slender fingers curving around the fabric in a move both needy and intimate—a move that did something to him he wasn't quite sure he should like *quite* so much.

Pearly-white teeth sank into the soft swell of her bottom lip before pulling free and he stopped breathing altogether.

"Megan."

She sighed. "I'm starving."

For a beat he stared down at her. And then those fingers tightened and she gave his lapel a little shake. *"Star-ving."*

A single nod.

Food.

Yeah, he was pretty hungry too. For something, anyway. So it was time to stop staring down into her pretty, freckle-kissed face.

"Right." Downing the rest of his glass in one swallow, he handed off the empty to a passing server. "Then I'm your man."

Seven hours earlier...

He'd thought it couldn't get any better than the laugh. But then he'd heard the laugh coupled with the squeals of delight and gotten an eyeful of Megan's sensational and perfectly displayed backside. Shimmying in some victory dance as her winning machine counted up at the far end of the waffle buffet their surprisingly reliable cabbie had recommended.

Damn.

She'd caught him by surprise. Again. Lulling him into too easy a conversation and then giving up the details of her life as easily as this machine had given up her winnings. All it had taken was the right question at the right time, and she'd opened up, revealing new insight into the engaging creature he'd managed to capture for the night.

She was a self-proclaimed recovering romantic. A woman who believed in love but had discovered through a lifetime of experience the heights of that particular romantic elevation to be beyond her reach. And she'd accepted it, wasn't interested in the futility of an unattainable pursuit. She was a brainiac beauty. A freelance software engineer, successful in her own right. Confident where it counted and modest in the most appealing ways. Independent to an extreme and unafraid to buck convention when it came to the achievement of her goals. Kind, funny and sexy.

Now he stood behind her, their latest round of cocktails set aside—which maybe wasn't such a bad thing considering the kind of detours his head had been taking—as he shrugged out of his suit jacket, giving in to the absurdly out-of-place bit of possessive insanity going nuts thinking about anyone else seeing this heart-shaped perfection.

"Here, put this on," he said, slipping it over her shoulders.

"I can't believe it!" she gasped. "I never win. I never, ever, *ever* get lucky like this."

Connor grinned, watching as the bare length of her arms disappeared within the sea of his coat. Reaching over, he adjusted the lapels, telling himself she'd looked cold. Then before he gave in to the temptation to linger near that tantalizing V of feminine flesh, or God forbid let his knuckles skim the softness there, he moved on to cuff her sleeves. Rolling up the arms until the slim band of her wristwatch shone beneath the flashing lights of her winning machine. It was a delicate band, but a little plain. The way he'd mistakenly thought about her, when really this girl glittered like a diamond.

"Carter," she said breathlessly, those blue eyes watching where his thumb stroked across the sensitive pale skin of her inner wrist.

"Connor." What the hell was he doing?

Her eyes lifted slowly, following the line of his arm, across his shoulder, to the top of his tie and then his mouth.

Did she have any idea how seductive those few beats of time were when he could all but see her mind working through the possibilities of where her gaze lingered.

This woman was hot. And sweet. And smart. And funny.

And she was staring at his mouth like it looked better than vanilla vodka and white-chocolate liqueur.

Like maybe, after all, she might want a taste.

Or even more.

Another beat and her eyes met his.

"Connor," she corrected, the good judgment wrestling in those blue pools, barely holding out against temptation.

Damn, he liked the way she said his name. Especially when she got it right.

He had an excellent idea for helping her remember too.

Repetition. And positive reinforcement—the breathless, moaning, pleading kind.

Hours of it.

He could push—turn on the seduction and he'd have her.

This flirtation he'd been playing at was nothing. For every

easy compliment, he'd kept a physical space between them. For every suggestive line, he'd avoided eye contact. Because he'd known—had a sense about what could be between them, and he'd steered clear of it. Only, now…he wanted more.

Shaking his head, he glared at the half-empty glass on the counter beside them. *Your fault.*

Pushing those thoughts aside, he put the arm's length back between them, the easy smile. The just-for-fun.

Moments later they were outside in the night air, surrounded by the bright lights, the drifting foot traffic and steady stream of cars. "You just cracked two machines in a row. We ought to head back to the casino and find you a real jackpot. Or would you like to try something different, like roulette?"

A deep sigh left her pretty mouth. "I don't think so. For someone who doesn't win very often, I'm happy to be coming out ahead the way I am. I don't want to push my luck."

"Something else in mind?" he asked. But he already knew, having seen the flash of resignation in her eyes.

Goodbye.

He didn't want the night to end, but she had a plan, after all. He respected her for it. Admired the sense of priority, forethought and commitment she'd put into it. Hell, that plan was probably half her appeal.

"I've had a really good time tonight." Megan shifted in front of him, her gaze skating away as her fingers slid down the lapels of his suit jacket, to where they idly played with the top button.

"Me too. Of course, this is Vegas. It's still early."

Her eyes pulled back to his, flickering only once to his mouth. "Early morning."

And then her shoulders were straightening, her features falling into an altogether too-polite expression. "And I've got a big day ahead of me."

"Big day of attending."

"Yes. And making up elaborate lies about our night together." This time her grin was pure imp. "Give Jodie and Tina something juicier to chew on than each other."

"Wow, you're going to lie about me?" he asked, settling his

hand at the small of her back as they approached the curb in search of a cab. "I'm flattered."

Nothing available, but one would come along any minute.

Megan shot him a wry smile. "Actually, probably not. I want to. It would be so great. But lying gives me hives. Even for a good cause like keeping the peace at my cousin's wedding, I'm not sure I'd be able to do it."

"So you're one of those perpetually honest types?" he asked as they walked in the direction of the casino where they were staying.

"Pretty much. Not always convenient. But I guess it keeps me out of trouble most times."

Uh-huh, but if she didn't stop worrying that sexy bottom lip between her teeth—nothing would keep her out of the trouble he had in mind.

Only, then she noticed the way he was watching her, and looked away.

He didn't want to lose her attention. Not yet. "With women like Tina and Jodie, I'm thinking not saying anything at all would be as effective as telling them what a stallion I am—which, incidentally, is one hundred percent accurate. Leave them to stew in their curiosity. Speculate to their hearts' content. And give them nothing."

"Oooh, it'll drive them *insane*," she gasped, nearly bouncing beside him and making him wonder how deep her wicked streak went. And if it ever blurred the line into naughty. "God knows their imaginations are more colorful than mine."

Giving in to another smirk, he offered, "I could help with that."

He was joking. Mostly.

Megan stopped and shook her head, the straight ends of her hair brushing softly across her shoulders. "I'm sure you could."

Even beneath the lights and glitz of the Strip, he could see the rise of a deep blush in her cheeks, read all the subtle signs of hesitation as they came. He could see her talking herself out of every maybe, what-if, just-a-few-more and only-this-once idea popping into her pretty head. He could feel the tension as she wrestled with her conscience about extending a night they'd both enjoyed.

He knew she wanted to... "But you have a plan."

Honest. Intelligent. Funny. Independent. Megan was all that and more, with the kind of practical approach to love he couldn't get out of his head. Eyes to the sky, he pushed out a long breath—that stopped abruptly when his focus caught on the neon sign flashing over her right shoulder.

She had a plan...but maybe it wasn't the only one.

God, she didn't want the night to end. But there was only one place it could go. And as much as the idea of falling into this man's bed appealed to her, it wasn't how she lived her life.

It didn't matter that he seemed more soul mate than stranger. Or that she'd never be in a position to let go like this again. If she gave in, she'd regret it tomorrow.

And when she thought about this night, she didn't want there to be any regrets.

So she swallowed and did what she had to do. "I have a plan."

The words opened an emptiness inside her, different from the one that had been so much a part of her every day.

"Thank you for a wonderful evening, Carter."

His mouth tilted in another one of those unreadable half smiles.

Tempting. So tempting.

"Megan, about your plan." He caught her elbow in a loose hold. "There's one thing I'm curious about."

Facing him, she asked, "What's that?"

His fingers slipped from her elbow down her arm in a soft caress and, catching her hand in his, he tucked it low against her back. Stepped in and, dropping his stare to her mouth, murmured, "Just this."

And he kissed her.

At first, the shock of contact was all she could register. And then the slow, back-and-forth rub of his mouth against hers. The firm pressure. The gentle pull. The low-level current riding all the places they touched.

Yes.

Just this.

The perfect end to a night she wished didn't have to.

Seconds later there was a breath between them—passing back and forth in a soft wash of warm and wet.

"Connor," he murmured, close enough she could almost feel the vibration on her lips.

Megan blinked, but didn't step back as she peered up into his eyes. "What?"

The corner of his mouth tipped. "Wanted to make sure you remembered my name."

"Connor." She sighed, closing her eyes to savor the moment just a little longer before she left. "That was very nice."

Catching her with a crooked finger beneath her chin, Connor brought her gaze back to his. When their eyes met, she had to blink. It wasn't the bittersweet sort of resigned longing *she felt* that was shining in his eyes. Not by a long shot. It was cocky arrogance and a sharply focused anticipation.

"Not really," he said, curving his hand so it cupped her jaw. "*That* was getting you used to the idea."

Her lips parted to protest, but before she had the chance to backtrack or reword her response, he'd swooped in again. Closing the bit of distance between them without hesitation. Taking her mouth as if it was his to do with as he pleased, making it his own in a way that had Megan's hands rising of their own volition, her fingers curling into his tailored shirt, her moan sliding free of her mouth and into his. There wasn't anything even remotely *nice* about this kiss. It was hot. Explosive. Consuming and intense.

It was the kind of kiss for behind closed doors. The kind she'd never in her life believed she would have allowed to take place in the middle of a crowded sidewalk. But then, she'd never been faced with the need to break away from something so damn good.

And then she wasn't thinking about what she should be doing at all. Where she was. Or where she was going. There was only the hot press of Connor's body as he pulled her closer. The skillful exploration of a part of her that suddenly felt like undiscovered country. The slow lick of his tongue against hers.

Delicious.

So good.

Another wicked lick was followed by a slow, steady thrust, and she was lost to it. Her hands moved against the hard planes of his torso in restless anticipation of what more he could give her.

She might regret this tomorrow…but not nearly as much as she would regret walking away tonight.

When Connor pulled back, she was breathless. Hungry. Desperate.

This time, the elusive tilt to Connor's lips was gone. He drew a slow breath, his brows seeming to draw lower through every passing second until his eyes had become fathomless depths, so dark she wondered if, once she fell in, she'd ever make it back out again.

"Okay, yeah," he murmured, as though having reached some internal understanding with himself.

"Yeah, okay," she whispered, nodding. "But we have to go back to your room. I'm sharing a suite with Tina and Jodie."

Only, then his head lowered to hers, and he pressed a single slow kiss against her lips before moving close to her ear. "I've got an even better idea."

A second later his hands had clamped around her hips and she'd been hoisted over his shoulder, where she bounced with his long strides. Delighted by this show of caveman antics, she breathlessly laughed out a demand for an explanation.

"I've got a plan…" he answered, confident and excited. "I'll tell you about it on the way. It's up here on the right."

CHAPTER FOUR

THE QUIET HUM OF THE SHOWER came to a stop, leaving only the silence of the villa roaring around him. Connor stared out over the bedroom terrace and private Caribbean blue pool below, trying to anticipate what he would face when his wife emerged from her steamy refuge.

Megan had held it together through those first minutes of realization, even managing a few joking remarks between bouts of nausea—but as soon as she'd been strong enough to stand on her own, she'd asked for some privacy to clean up.

And he'd been waiting since. Listening to the lock snap on the bathroom door as it closed behind him. Contemplating the single muted sob he'd heard before the echoing spray of the shower drowned all other sound. Piecing together the events, revelations and resolutions of the night before. Trying to reconcile them with the here and now of the morning.

Megan wanted a lawyer.

It had been the only definitive statement she'd made regarding their marriage in those few chaotic moments they'd spent ensconced in their marble-and-brass hideaway. Granted, she was probably as hazy on the finer points of the night as he was, but something possessive inside him was growling in outrage at the thought.

She was his wife.

She'd married him. And not on some lark either, but because she'd recognized the potential between them, same as him.

So yeah, the alcohol may have played into the immediacy of

his actions. But with every passing minute, the details of those critical hours they'd spent together and the woman he'd married sharpened in his mind, reaffirming his confidence in the decision to strike while the iron was hot.

And no, the irony wasn't lost on him that after his patient, methodical approach to finding a wife had failed with Caro— Megan had just dropped into his lap. Sure, sure, he'd had to sell her on the idea once he'd seen the sense in it. But he was a man with a knack for identifying opportunity and the skills to convey the benefits of said opportunity to others. He could size up a situation and break down the key factors, without waiting for the proverbial knock at his door or encyclopedic pitch most people required prior to taking action. And what he'd seen in Megan told him she was the kind of opportunity he shouldn't kick out of his bed for eating crackers— or, more specifically, downing half Nevada's monthly import of vanilla vodka in one night.

Their agendas were simply too well aligned to ignore. The timing too right. The practical approach too perfect. And she'd been like-minded enough to see it and agree.

Megan fit him to a T, so he wasn't prepared to admit he'd made a mistake. Not yet anyway. Though he supposed the next few minutes would be fairly telling on that count. A bout of hysterics, for instance, would most definitely have him reconsidering his stance.

The lock released with a loud click and Connor steeled his gut for what came next. Only, somehow the sight of Megan, towel dried, freshly scrubbed and swimming in a thick, oatmeal robe as she tentatively pushed a damp tendril from her brow, was something he had no defense against.

She was beautiful.

And the steady way she met his eyes proved she wasn't a meltdown in progress. Though taking the rest of her body language into account—the crossed arms, one hand securing the overlap of panels high at her neck and the other wrapped tight around her waist—suggested she wasn't quite ready to pick up where they'd left off the night before. She looked cautious. Alert. And cool.

She looked strong, and it had his pulse jacking as much as the sight of those sexy little pink toenails peeking out from beneath the hem of her oversize robe.

"Feeling better?" he asked, planting a shoulder against the sliding door rather than giving in to the urge to get closer. He wanted her comfortable. As quickly as he could make it happen.

"Yes, thank you." Clearing her throat quietly, she glanced briefly around before returning her attention to him. "I needed that. Needed a few minutes to get my thoughts together. I'm sorry to have kept you waiting out here, though."

Conscientious. Nice. "Not a problem. It's been an interesting morning, and it started off a little faster than I think either one of us expected."

Her brows lifted as she drew a long breath. "It did, but considering our situation, that's probably for the best. We've got a lot to cover in a short time."

And then before he had a chance to ask, that steady gaze filled with purpose and her thumb popped up like a bullet point as she began.

"So, we'll both need a lawyer to navigate the legalities involved in granting an annulment. But I'd be willing to bet the front desk has at least some cursory information available about the process, this being Vegas and all. I'll ask when I run down to make copies of whatever documentation we got from the... chapel?"

Connor offered a short nod, his frown deepening as she ticked off to-dos with her fingers.

Independent. He admired it...but she was working in the wrong direction. Megan had made it to four before he'd pushed off the wall and caught her slender hand in his own. "Hey, slow down a second."

Her breath caught and her eyes went wide. "The fourth was this," she said, her voice coming quieter as she wiggled the offending digit in his grasp. "Your ring. I was afraid to take it off until I could give it back to you."

Connor's brow furrowed as she began to slide the platinum-and-diamond-set band free.

"Wait. Let me look at it on your hand."

Her gaze lifted to his, questioning and wary.

"It looks good on you." Worth every considerable grand he'd sunk into it the night before.

Megan nodded, the corner of her mouth curving in quiet appreciation. "The most stunning ring I've ever seen. I wish I could remember more than how incredibly it sparkled beneath the fluorescent lights in the wedding-chapel bathroom."

Connor let out a low chuckle, playing with the band where it sat on her finger. And then stopped, suddenly not finding her words funny at all.

Staring down at the little crease working its way between her brows, he asked, "Megan, you don't remember me buying you this ring?"

She swallowed, and the crease deepened. "You can't even imagine how much I wish I did. But no. I don't actually—" Seeming to think better of it, she cut off her words with a shake of her head. "It doesn't matter."

Like hell. "Megan, it matters to me. Do you remember when I asked you?"

"No." Not a blink, not a waver.

"The wedding?"

"I'm sorry. No."

Connor stared at her, his mind stalled on the seeming impossibility of what he was hearing. Yeah, she'd obviously had a few too many—they both had. Hell, he'd been hit hard enough where more than a few minutes had been required for the details to shuffle into place, and he probably had at least seventy-five pounds on her...but blacking out?

"Megan," he started, working to keep the urgency out of his voice. "Exactly how much of last night *do* you remember?"

"A few minutes here and there."

Alarm spreading through him like wildfire, he waited for her to say something more. Waited for her to finish her sentence with "seem to be missing." Only, then the ring was free, being pressed into his palm, wrapped tight beneath fingers

Megan had dutifully closed for him. And she was peering up at him, those blue pools searching his eyes for something… anything maybe.

"I remember seeing you at a bar and thinking how handsome you were. I remember laughing…a lot, and at another point, talking over waffles, though about what I couldn't say except you looked serious then. I remember you joking about us picking out china patterns. And I remember knowing with all certainty you weren't serious. There weren't any maybes between us. It simply wasn't like that." Her cheeks turned a delicate shade of pink as she looked away. "I remember knowing I should slow down because I don't really drink much, but ordering another round because I didn't want the fun to end. And I remember signing my name in the chapel, thinking—God, I don't even know what. So, I guess, not really thinking at all."

Connor stared, stunned as she turned away, a flush still blazing in her cheeks even as her shoulders remained straight. The air left his lungs on a hot expletive as he watched her nudge at the decorative pillows and shams littering the floor around the bed with her foot.

No wonder she was treating their marriage like some throwaway Vegas souvenir. This woman had a plan, and she didn't remember a single one of the reasons Connor had given her for changing it. Hell, she barely remembered him. And yet, she'd somehow managed to hold it together, remaining calm and focused throughout.

She was strong. Tough.

Everything he wanted.

Her mouth pulled to the side. "I don't suppose you happen to know where I might find my dress?"

Images of that superfine, silky bit of blue hitting him in the face flashed through his mind; only, where the dress went after had been as low a priority then as it was now.

"Megan. I'm sorry. If I'd realized, I would have been telling you everything, trying to fill in the night, explaining what happened. Why didn't you ask?"

* * *

Closing her eyes, Megan drew a steadying breath.

Why? Because the details weren't important and she could decipher the broad strokes on her own. This gorgeous, carefree guy had tempted her with all the things she'd sworn she could live without...the attention of a charming, desirable man, the chance to be utterly spontaneous, the indulgence in a night of reckless excess she wouldn't even consider once she had another person dependent on her. And so her pickled mind had rationalized this one last adventure. Vegas-style.

Maybe her blocking out their time together was some sort of defense mechanism.

Looking at this man alone made her believe whatever happened between them could very well have been the kind of phenomenal a grown woman didn't recover from, and her inner psyche was simply trying to protect her.

"Megan?" The deep, rich baritone cut into her thoughts an instant before the heat of his hands settled over her shoulders, jolting her back to the now. "Why?"

"It doesn't matter."

And then those strong hands were turning her around, gripping her tight. "You're wrong. I don't think you understand. Last night wasn't just some goof to be rectified this morning."

She blinked, trying to look away even as she felt herself stumbling further into the intensity of Connor's dark eyes. He thought there was something meaningful between them? Some potential?

This wasn't what she needed to hear.

"It has to be." She couldn't invest in potential again. She didn't have the time and she didn't have the will. "I have a plan."

She'd expected him to back off a step, ask what she was talking about, but instead that single corner of his mouth turned up to the slightest degree. As if suddenly he found himself on better footing than he'd expected. "Yeah, but my plan's better. Even you think so."

She'd told him?

Her chin pulled back as she felt the sting of self-betrayal and cursed her inner psyche.

Was nothing sacred?

Images of the laughter came back to her in a sickening rush, and she couldn't help but wonder if all her goals and intentions had been a part of the joke. Only, as she looked into Connor's eyes, some instinctive part of her knew it wasn't the case.

So what, then…

"Oh, my God." Her throat closed tight, trying to strangle the words she didn't want to say. "Did you volunteer to be my sperm donor?"

He was tall and handsome, without any obvious festering infections—

"No." His brows, already drawn low over his eyes, went even lower, obscuring what little chance she'd had to try to read a man who wasn't exactly an open book to begin with. "Not really. Not like you're thinking."

Not like she was thinking? Like what, then? she thought with a fresh wave of panic.

Her eyes fell to the empty spot on her ring finger. He'd married her. So maybe it wasn't so much a donation at all. Donations were free and clear…and this guy had already tied her down with a fairly significant string.

He wanted dibs on her baby.

He wanted a claim.

Suddenly, her breath was coming faster than it should, and the air working its way in and out of her lungs felt thin and useless.

"Wait, Megan. I don't know what you're thinking, but I can tell from your face it's wrong. Let me explain."

"You're gay." What else would a guy who looked like this be doing with her?

"Uh…" That tilted smile was back and she knew she was right.

"Okay, so you don't want your parents to know? You need an heir or something to keep your trust fund?"

"No—uh—I—uh—"

Shaking her head, she closed her eyes. "Look, Carter, either way, it doesn't matter. Whatever deal we might have worked out last night is off."

She'd been heavily intoxicated. Even if she'd signed a dozen documents, they would never stand up. She could walk away, unless—

Her eyes shot wide as she stared up at him in horror. "Did you…try…to get me pregnant last night?"

Connor coughed, his amused expression morphing into shock, confusion and something she really, really didn't want to believe was guilt no matter how much it looked like it.

His hand came up between them, but she didn't care if he needed a minute to sort out his story or work through his defense. Spinning away, she banded her arms across her abdomen, sick with the knowledge of what she'd done. "Of all the stupid, self-sabotaging, dangerous—"

"Megan." The way he said her name made it half plea, half laugh.

What had she done? Even if she wasn't pregnant, she'd had unprotected sex with a man she didn't know.

…patient zero…

Her stomach pitched hard. "He could have an STD," she gasped, her own anxiety pushing the words past her lips before she'd thought to stifle them.

"Megan." This time her name sounded strained coming through his lips. As though this guy was losing his patience.

Tough. Whatever he was thinking, he'd have to put a pin in it. She had bigger fish to fry than worrying about his patience when her best-case scenario was not pregnant, not infected, but still having to push back her plan by six months to ensure enough time for any STDs to show up in the screen.

"Damn it, Megan, look at me." Those hands were on her again, spinning her around and holding her still as Connor got in her face.

"One." He let go of her to bring his thumb up. "I do not have any sexually transmitted diseases. I always use a condom and following the breakup of my yearlong committed relationship had myself tested, as a precaution, regardless. Two." His index finger was next. "Neither is there a trust fund nor some executor to appease regarding it. Every cent I have, I earned on my own. Three, where the hell do you get this stuff?" Another finger. "Four, I didn't marry you to get my hands on a baby. I married you because we had similar goals and priorities and expectations…and damn it, I married you because I liked you a hell of a lot too."

She shook her head, searching those impossible eyes. "But it doesn't make sense—"

He waved her off. "And five, I absolutely did not try to get you pregnant last night. We didn't have sex."

Her jaw dropped.

So he was gay.

And why the revelation hit her like disappointment when she ought to be turning cartwheels, she couldn't say. But she'd deal with it later.

Only. then that mishmash of backward thinking was in play again, rising up with a victorious laugh at a thought that should have spurred outrage. "But I was *naked*," she challenged, recalling she'd literally stumbled over her panties and hideous T-shirt sprinting to the bathroom. A lucky break considering how fast on her heels Connor had been.

Naked *and* puking would have been a low she didn't care to contemplate.

"Yeah, and I didn't say *nothing* happened." With that concession, his gaze burned a slow path down her body, leaving her with the sense the bulk of her robe was all but invisible. He'd seen her before. And right then, he was seeing her again.

"Connor!"

His eyes met hers, completely unrepentant. "Man, I love it when you get my name right."

"Wait…what?"

"Say it again for me."

"Okay," she swallowed. "I believe you. You're probably not gay."

"Mmm. So sure?" he needled.

Make that *definitely* not. Like they *definitely* should have
steered clear of the topic of sex altogether. Because having
touched on it, now those hard-to-read eyes of his weren't so
hard to read at all. They were filled with a possessive sort of
predatory heat...directed at her.

"I could convince you. Spend the next hour or two making
my argument." Leaning into her space, he added, "I'm a pretty
compelling guy when I set my mind to it."

"Connor," she warned, trying not to give in to the laugh
threatening to escape. She should be horrified. Traumatized.
So why was it, in the aftermath of the worst decision of her life,
this man's totally inappropriate taunts and teasing were somehow making her feel safe.

As if he'd sensed the ease in her tension, something changed
in the man before her. The joking and pretense were set aside.
Connor was completely serious, and her soul-deep awareness
of his shift in mood was more disconcerting than waking up
next to a stranger had been.

"Megan, the reason we didn't have sex last night was because you went from laughing and sexy and totally in the moment to not feeling so great. So instead of taking you to bed, I
put you there. Simple."

Simple. Somehow it didn't feel that way.

He took her hand. "I should have realized how much you'd
had to drink. I should have stopped us earlier."

"I'm a big girl with better sense than this. I should have
stopped myself. Obviously." She drew a slow breath and pressed
the heels of her hands against the dull throb at her temples.
"Look at where it got me."

"Married." Connor's warm palm cupped her cheek as he
searched her eyes, his elusive smile nowhere to be found. "To
a man who's about as perfect an alternative to your plan as you
can get. And you don't even remember why."

"But you do?" she asked, the quiet words sounding too sincere for the sarcastic tone she'd intended.

Suddenly she wanted that only-half-the-story smirk back,
because this straightforward intensity she could actually *feel*

thrumming through the air between them, pulsing against her skin as if it was trying to get inside, was too much to bear.

He was a stranger. Only, this stranger was looking into her eyes as if he knew exactly who she was.

"More every minute."

CHAPTER FIVE

MEGAN'S LIPS WERE PARTED, revealing that bit of wet just beyond the pale swell he wanted to run his thumb across. But Megan didn't remember him. Which meant, though she'd taken vows, signed her name, worn his ring and climbed all over him the night before…this morning, she didn't belong to him.

He understood it.

Accepted it.

Only, when she looked into his eyes the way she was now. When her breathing changed the smallest degree, and the color morning had leached from her skin pushed back into her cheeks, it felt an awful lot like she was.

Like on some level she knew what they'd had between them. And wanted it again.

He could show her how it had been. Kiss her until they were both senseless and she was begging him like she had—

Her breath caught. "I should find my dress."

Or he could wait. Damn it.

Moving back, Connor shoved his hands into his pockets.

Those big blue eyes were crawling away again, scanning the space around them as though salvation could be found in some dark corner of the room. Only, then they brightened as a small squeak escaped her, and Connor realized she'd found her dress.

"Thank God. I figure I pretty well earned this walk of shame, but seriously, I didn't want to have to do it in a robe."

Again Connor felt a smile pushing at his lips. She had a sense of humor. One he appreciated.

"Walk of shame, eh. I don't know if married women qualify."

Megan cringed at the words he'd been trying out on his tongue. Testing the feel of in his mouth.

They hadn't been bad or bitter or totally out of place, and he wondered if they might be an acquired taste he was warming up to. Something to encourage his wife to try.

Megan worried her bottom lip. "Looking at this dress, I definitely qualify."

As sexy and smooth as it had been draped over her curves the night before, the wrinkled garment barely ranked above a rag this morning.

"I can call down to the concierge and get you one sent up—"

Megan choked, "Wait, don't—I'll wear one of your shirts or something"

"I like the idea of you wrapped up in one of my shirts...quite a lot. But first let's have breakfast."

This time it was Megan at a loss for words, and he savored it for the full second and a half he had before she'd found her new tack. "I can't stay for breakfast. I've got a wedding today. A real wedding."

Connor stiffened. "As opposed to the fake—and yet legally binding—variety from last night."

Apologetic eyes drifted back to him. "I only meant—"

He put up a hand, waving off her apology. "I know what you meant. One they'd planned. And I know you're freaked out and more than a little desperate to get out of here and collect your thoughts, but, Megan, we're married. We need to discuss this. You've got hours before Gail's expecting you. We'll have some food to settle your stomach. Talk. Call it a—getting-to-know-your-husband date?" At her hesitation, he asked, "Come on, you're too much of a control freak not to have questions."

The look in her eyes said it all. She had a million of them. But there was more than curiosity in those crystal depths. There was fear, as well. As if somehow, she was afraid of what she might learn.

"Megan, come on. I can't be *that* bad."

"I don't think you're bad. I'm just confused and overwhelmed and…" She squared her shoulders. "I'm not entirely sure a getting-to-know-you anything makes much sense, all things considered."

All things considered.

Code for the lawyers again. Divorce.

Connor cocked his jaw to the left and crossed his arms, looking hard at the woman he'd married the night before.

No doubt a divorce would be the simplest solution.

He could let her go. Put a couple of his lawyers on it, have the whole situation resolved quietly and quickly.

She didn't remember him. Them.

So really it would almost be as if the whole thing never happened.

Except he'd remember. He'd know.

Putting up a shrug, Connor made a decent show of nonchalance as he pulled the ace from his sleeve. "Yeah, you're probably right. Besides, if you need to talk, I'm sure Jodie and Tina would be happy to lend an ear. You've got, what, four hours to kill before they get their hands on another distraction?"

Megan's startled gaze snapped to his. "Do they know?"

Oh, yeah, wifey wasn't going anywhere. Not for a while, anyway.

"They know you and I left the bar together. And you didn't come back to the suite you were sharing last night. So I'd say they know enough to make me the lesser evil on option this morning."

"The lesser evil?" Her brow quirked, leaving her mouth to hint at the smile and laughter that had gotten them into this mess. "Wow, you sure know how to sell yourself."

Making him want more.

"Don't have to," he said, crossing the bedroom. "Not when I'm up against those two."

Her stare narrowed on him as she followed. "Fine. You win. Let's play getting-to-know-you."

Connor did his best to rein in the victorious grin working over his mouth, and swung open the bedroom door.

The master suite was situated at the end of the second-level hall, overlooking the main living space where marble and glass gleamed in contrast to rich jewel-toned fabrics, heavily carved wood and silk-covered walls.

Megan's steps faltered, the shock on her face this morning even better than it had been the night before.

"So, Megan. The first thing you should know about me…"

"Uh-huh, yes?"

"I don't want a divorce."

"Just give it a try?" Megan asked, sputtering at the insanity of Connor's suggestion, casually tossed out as he'd perused an elaborate breakfast spread in the dining room. "You're crazy."

Glancing up from the coffee he'd stirred a generous portion of cream into, he grinned. "Exactly what you said last night. Of course, there'd been a whole lot of breathless 'yes, please' tied up in 'you're crazy' then."

Her eyes rolled skyward. She could only imagine the circumstances. Didn't want to imagine them. But couldn't seem to help it. In fact, every time her gaze touched on those criminally captivating lips…she started imagining all over again. Imagining, but not remembering.

"Last night I was forty percent alcohol by volume. Last night doesn't count."

Another shrug. "It counts to me. And if you'll sit down and have something to eat, I'll tell you why it counts to you too."

Handing her the coffee, he nodded at the tray of pastries, fresh fruit, cheeses and breads he'd brought to the table. "Trust me on this, you want the food in your stomach first."

Connor selected a croissant, set it, a tiny ceramic crock of butter and another of jam on a china plate with a silver knife, and pushed it in front of her. "Eat."

She looked at it warily, not really wanting to eat anything at all after the way her morning had begun.

She was nervous. Frustrated. And more than a smidgen concerned about Connor's apparent commitment to this monumental mistake.

He didn't want a divorce. She didn't get it. It didn't make sense.

"You don't know me," she began with a slow shake of her head. "Even if I'd talked your ear off from the minute we met until my little pilgrimage to the porcelain god...you couldn't really know me. My beliefs, my hang-ups, my shortcomings."

Connor heaved a sigh and met her eyes. "I know you wanted a conventional family, and I know, while you're friends with the men you date, you've never actually fallen in love. Same as me, that fairy-tale connection people go after like junkies looking for their next fix isn't a part of your makeup. I know you're tired of making yourself vulnerable again and again, hoping each time things will end differently. And I know you've figured out what you really want is a child, and you don't need a husband to get one."

Okay, so maybe he knew her a little.

Megan sat back in her chair, watching this virtual stranger reach for her plate, rip a corner off her croissant, butter it and, as though he hadn't just relayed her deepest secret and greatest failures, hold it out in offering.

"Eat, while I clear a few things up between us."

Tentatively she took the bite, letting the flakes of rich, buttery pastry dissolve on her tongue.

"For the record, I've been interested in settling down for some time. But contrary to what the evidence might suggest, marriage isn't something I take lightly or would jump into without serious consideration."

When she opened her mouth to call him on that last bit, he lifted a staying hand and went on.

"Marriage is the foundation of a family, and I want mine to be rock solid. I want the security—for my children, and really us both as well—of knowing it won't crumble under some needy, emotional pique or the whims of a fickle heart. So I've been waiting for a woman with a specific sense of priority."

His brow pulled down as he stared at the table and then looked back to her with a knowing expression. "And before you start thinking I was just some man on the make last night, out trawling for a wife, I wasn't. I wasn't looking for anything but the good time we were having. And then, it just hit me. You were the one."

"The one." There was a whole lot of weight in that statement. More than she'd expected to be shouldering through this weekend trip to Vegas.

"Yes. Now, let me tell you how much I respect your plan to prioritize your child over the instinct to find a mate."

She gulped.

Wow, if she'd told him that, she'd really told him everything.

"It takes time to build a relationship. If you have a child, it's time you'll be taking away from him or her. And what if it gets serious?" he asked, buttering another small piece of croissant. "You introduce little Megan to this guy, but then it doesn't work out. Now you aren't the only one who's let down. It's your daughter or son, as well. Plus, there's the whole post-breakup emotional slump to contend with. No picnic for a single mom, or the little person more in tune with her feelings than anyone else on the planet. That this isn't the kind of emotional cycling you want your child to go through says a tremendous amount about you. And, like I said, I respect it."

He'd spoken casually, seemingly at ease, and yet there was an intensity about him as he relayed this bit of perspective on her plan that implied a level of empathy beyond what she'd expect.

A part of her wanted to ask him about his past. About his parents. Things she wondered if they'd discussed the night before. Only, to do so would open more doors, and she was already confused enough without adding images of this powerful man as a vulnerable child to the mix.

Connor reached out to offer her the next bite and she caught his wrist in her hand. "I don't understand. If you respect my plan so much, how did we end up married?"

Those dark eyes held with hers. "Because what I offered you was the best of both worlds without the risk of the worst."

"How?"

"Simple. This thing between us, Megan. It's not about love."

Her chin pulled back as she absorbed the words. Felt them

wash through her with the same kind of phantom familiarity she'd been experiencing on and off with Connor since she'd woken in his bed. Only, this time, something about it wasn't entirely comforting. Almost like a piece of the puzzle that was her missing experience had been put into place sideways and didn't quite fit.

Maybe it simply wasn't what she'd expected him to say, though why not, she didn't know. Surely she hadn't believed this man who married her within hours of their meeting had *fallen in love* with her. Talk about crazy. Still, somehow hearing him say it left her feeling...confused.

So she asked, "If it's not about love, then what?"

Connor gave her a satisfied grin. "All the vital components that make a relationship successful, without any of the emotional messiness to drag it down. It's about respect, caring and commitment. Shared goals and compatible priorities. It's about treating a marriage like a partnership instead of some romantic fantasy. It's about two people *liking* each other."

Liking each other. What this man was suggesting was what she'd had in most every relationship she'd attempted. With one major difference. In those relationships, neither she nor the man she'd been dating believed it was enough. Whereas with Connor... "So, you're saying it's about expectations. If we limit them, no one's disappointed."

"Embrace them," he corrected, "because they work for us."

She nodded, saying the words slowly. "A partnership."

Of course, this man wouldn't want anything more from her.

He frowned as he met her eyes. "I'm not talking about some relationship without any caring. I'm talking about improving on friendship. Without turning it into something neither of us is capable of delivering on."

"If what you're looking for is a friend, surely, Connor, you must have hundreds to choose from. Women you know better. Trust more. Women who want this."

Connor stared at her a moment, considering his words before he spoke them. "But I want you. The truth is, there isn't another woman I know better. At least not as it applies to core beliefs and priorities. You didn't have some ulterior motive when we met. You didn't know who I was or what I had or what you thought I wanted. In fact, from the start, the most consistent thing about you has been your unwavering honesty, even when it didn't suit your needs. I got to know the you who *didn't* want a relationship. I like what I've learned about you, Megan. The independence. The sharp wit. The easy laugh and intelligent conversation. The authenticity.

"Sure, the historical events that made you the woman you are today are still a mystery, but what you want and who you are and how we get along... Those things I know. I like."

She swallowed. "Because of last night."

It didn't seem enough.

"Last night. This morning. Right this minute. I like what I see."

"So even if I am the kind of woman you're looking for..."

"*The* woman."

She nodded, feeling more uncertain than she had since waking with no memory. "What makes you the man for me?"

"I can take care of you."

"I can take care of myself."

"I know," he said, that wry twist in motion again. "It's one of the many, many things I appreciate about you. You're independent and self-sufficient. Your happiness won't be contingent on the amount of attention I can give you any given week. But as fully capable as you are, my support would allow you to be more than a single parent, with a single income. Married to me, you can be a full-time mother instead of a slave to the workforce. You can work or not work, whatever you choose. I have housekeepers, so any time you want to yourself won't be spent scrubbing grout. My work requires travel. You and our children would be encouraged to accompany me. You could see the world. Meet new people. There would be little, if anything, tying you down beyond the few expectations I have for my wife."

The muscles along her shoulders pulled tight. "What expectations?"

"There's a significant social element in my business, and I want a wife who can help balance the conversation. Playing hostess and accompanying me as needed for whatever comes up. Dinners, parties, charitable events. No more than a couple times a week. Also, our children—as many as you'd like—come first. They need to be your number-one priority. And lastly it means respecting both me and our marriage vows."

She understood. "Fidelity."

"Fidelity."

No surprise Connor wasn't the kind of man to sit idly while his wife entertained herself with the golf pro from the club, but within the marriage…

Her eyes drifted to where her hand was wrapped halfway around his wrist. She'd been touching him all this time, and yet this was the first moment she'd been aware of the low charge running between them. Meeting his gaze, she could see in those dark pools an answering awareness of that connection.

Her breath caught.

"You won't be lonely with me, Megan. I know what I'm suggesting doesn't follow the norm. It's not the traditional courtship and promise of love. But we aren't the most traditional people." Reversing her hold, he took her hand in his. "We have something good. All I'm asking is for you to give it a chance."

A chance.

She believed it could be good. Which was part of the problem. Because something good would be hard to lose.

And she'd lost so many times already. It was why she'd come up with the plan. No more waiting for the other shoe to drop. Hoping for something that would never come.

Except with Connor, love wasn't part of the equation. He simply wanted a partner. Someone who understood his priorities the way he understood hers.

He wanted to be another parent for their *children*.

As many as she wanted.

She'd always dreamed of a houseful of kids. But when she'd decided on the plan, she accepted in all likelihood there would be only the one. And one had been enough.

But what Connor was offering wasn't about *just enough*. He was offering her more than she'd believed she could wish for.

Still, the risk remained, reduced as it may be.

What if she got attached—let herself believe in a family—and he changed his mind? Left.

She couldn't go through it again.

"I need to think," she said, pushing back from the table and walking to the glass doors where the Vegas sun beat down, brutal and beautiful all at once, over their private oasis.

Moving in behind her, Connor rested his hands over her shoulders, pressing his thumbs into the tender muscles at either side of her spine. A part of her wanted to shrug him off, tell him to give her the space she asked for. But a bigger part recognized the act as an example of the kind of support he was offering. A subtle reminder she would not be alone. There would be someone behind her.

"I get it, Megan. I do. You don't remember and it's scary to take my word on something so huge." Then it wasn't merely the touch of his hands she was experiencing, but the press of his body along hers. His chin rested atop her head, his chest at her back as he continued rubbing the tension from her neck...and all she could think was how right it felt. "So I'm not asking you to believe in me right now. I'm asking you to believe in yourself."

She turned in his arms, her hands coming to rest on the planes of his chest as if it were the most natural thing in the word. "Believe in myself?"

Connor brushed his knuckles against her temple, soft and light.

"You married me. Don't you want to find out why?"

CHAPTER SIX

SHE'D AGREED.

Connor couldn't quite believe it himself—and yeah, yeah, it wasn't exactly the whole nine yards…more like a conservative six and half by his estimate—but Megan was spending the day with him. Giving him a chance to convince her of what kind of sense they made.

Which meant he was going to Gail's wedding. Fortunately, a Vegas-style seating chart had more to do with who got to the bar first than which great-aunt was too blind to figure out she'd scored a table by the kitchen.

Pouring another coffee for himself and a glass of juice for Megan, he listened with half an ear as she checked in with Gail. She'd barely gotten past hello before a suspicious silence, followed by some stuttering and then more silence, confirmed what he'd known from the start. Jodie and Tina had been running at the mouth, probably since Megan and he took off the night before.

"I did stay with him… Of course I'm fine, but that's not— Gail, you're getting married today— Yes, he is very handsome…"

This was the difference between men and women. When Connor texted Jeff to let him know something had come up and he'd get in touch next week, the guy had texted back a single word. Later. End of discussion. Granted, it might have gone longer if he'd mentioned the *something* in question was an exchange of vows, followed by a case of acute amnesia…but whatever.

"I know it's not like me... No, there weren't drugs involved—Stop! Gail, today is about you. When should I come by to help?"

Walking the juice over to the table, he set it down by her hand, running a thumb over her shoulder to make sure she saw it.

Then, covering the small of her back with his palm, he leaned close to her free ear. "Let me know if you need anything else."

Her eyes were wide when she turned slowly to look at him, and pure masculine satisfaction surged through him at the obvious impact his actions had spurred.

She *wanted* to be convinced.

"Wait, what?" she asked, her attention firmly back on the call at hand. "You don't want me—?"

Connor looked up, curious.

"Because of Jodie and Tina. Right... No, no, anything to make this day perfect for you."

She sounded uncertain but resigned. "Well, I'll see you down at the limo, then. And, Gail—could you get my bridesmaid dress sent over here?"

After a few more details were exchanged, Megan hung up and turned a hesitant smile his way. "Good news. We've got a few more hours to get to know each other."

"Oh, yeah?"

"Gail doesn't want to deal with Jodie and Tina while she's getting ready, and she can't have me if they aren't there, so we'll all meet at the limo when it's time to go."

"Come on over here," he said, patting the cushion beside him.

Megan crossed to him, a strained smile stiff on her lips, apprehension lurking in her eyes.

Good news his foot. She'd been banking on the break.

Taking her hand, he pulled her down beside him, leaving space between the crook of his knee and her hip, but keeping a light hold on her fingers. "Look, let's forget about all the reasons I'm such a stellar choice for a husband right now and relax. Talk."

Her eyes narrowed on his mouth and she pulled back the

slightest degree. "Why do I feel like you're about to sell me some snake oil?"

Connor didn't release her fingers, but tightened his hold, reeling her back in. "Because you're mildly pessimistic. Now, knock it off. You don't remember, but if there's one thing we do well...it's talk. About anything."

To prove his point, he picked up one of the papers delivered with breakfast and tossed it into Megan's lap. "So let's get this ball rolling. Check the headlines and then give me the first thing that comes to mind."

"You are so cheating!" Megan accused, her laughter doing little to back up the finger she jabbed at Connor's chest.

The finger he then grabbed and used to tow her off the knees she been perched on. And suddenly she was tucked in the small crease between Connor's half-sprawled form and the back of the couch. Again.

And again, she planted her palm on the center of his chest, refusing to admit how tempting it was to simply stay there, and pushed herself up.

Connor shook his head, all *who, me?* "Cheating? We're *talking.*"

She shot him a skeptical look, not buying his wide-eyed-innocent routine for one minute. That he would even try it with a mouth like his was almost too much to bear. "Sure we are. Talking about our views on education. A topic we have remarkably similar beliefs on."

Another wry smile twisted his lips. "So I'd like our kids to live at home, attending private school. And you agree. What's the problem?"

"Mmm-hmm. And before schooling, extreme-adventure sports. Funny topic to spring up out of the blue. And so coincidental you would be of the same mind regarding risks of that nature being off the table once a child enters the picture."

"I told you, we have a tremendous amount in common."

"Yeah, and you've worked it all into this 'casual' conversation over the last couple hours—"

"Come on, now, sweetheart, I've worked a lot of things into this conversation."

"—conveniently omitting anything we disagreed on."

Connor's mouth kicked up another degree, his eyes heating in the way she'd found so startling at first, but was now beginning to look for. "Have I mentioned how sexy those smarts of yours are?"

An unbidden belly flip had her glancing away before Connor could see how his words affected her. "I bust you for trying to play me, and this is your response?"

"Yes." The crook of his finger found her chin, and he pulled her back to his gaze. "But that doesn't make what we've talked about any less true. I'm a motivated guy, set on making sure I don't let something important slip through my fingers. I want you to know what I know."

She let out an even breath, hating the way everything Connor said made sense. Clicked, as if it was locking into some waiting place within her.

It was crazy to think, even for a second, about buying into this.

She'd sworn she wouldn't do it again. Wouldn't take another risk. And this…this was a risk unlike any she'd faced before. But staring into Connor's deep brown eyes, all she could think was, what if this time the reward was worth it?

A knock sounded from the front door, and Connor broke the eye contact to check his watch and then push up from the couch. "Got to be your dress."

A moment later a gleaming brass cart was parked in the entry and Connor was verifying the appointment for a stylist to do Megan's hair and makeup. She'd tried to stop him, but he'd dismissed her protests, calling it a perk of being Mrs. Reed…said she should get used to it. Or at the very least use it while she had it.

Fair enough. She'd given in. And now she had to admit she was looking forward to letting someone else work on her hair. In all honesty, her plate felt a little full already with the business of this marriage on it. And the herculean task of making her hair look good just wasn't something she had room for.

The door shut, and Connor, all tapered cut and balanced perfection, was closing in again. The skin along her shoulders began to tingle in reckless anticipation of that back-to-hard-chest-and-stomach stance he seemed to favor. And then he was there, running a thumb down the column of her neck. "Would you feel better if I shared a few points of dissent?"

Casting a glance over her shoulder, she saw his eyes were serious. And so close.

"Yes, I would."

Looking back at the dress before she turned around completely and did something monumentally stupid—which, considering her marital status, was really saying a lot—she pulled open the thin, protective plastic. Stroked her fingers over the silver, above-the-knee sheath.

Connor cleared his throat. "Camp."

She shot another look back. "What?"

"I don't like the idea of sending the kids away for extended periods of time."

"But camp's a treat. Once they're old enough, of course. They have so many incredible programs out there. Nature camps. Space camps—"

"Yeah, arts, football, gymnastics, and everything else a little boy or girl could be interested in." Shoving a hand through the dark silk of his hair, he let out a sigh. "I still don't like the idea, but I've given on the point already."

Her brows lifted along with the corners of her mouth as she turned to face him completely. "Wow. Any other small victories I should know about?"

"Christmas at home. Every year. All of us. Period."

She let out a small gasp, her hand moving to her heart in genuine shock. "You fought against…Christmas?"

Those dark eyes softened, crinkling at the corners. "Please wipe the 'he hates puppies' look off your face. I didn't want to count out a trip somewhere exotic. But your arguments were compelling, so it was a compromise easy to make."

Wow, he was so—

Wait.

Her eyes narrowed on him. "And now you're showing me how *reasonable* you are with all your willing concessions. Do you ever stop?"

Yes, she was fully aware of just how *unreasonable* her response to this man giving her exactly what she'd asked for was. But based on the twisted smile playing on his lips, Connor didn't seem to mind.

"Not until I get what I want."

She was getting lost in his eyes, feeling herself drawn closer with every minute they spent together. "And you want me."

Connor leaned in, closing the distance between them until the heat of his body was licking over hers. She swayed, suddenly breathless. The palm of his left hand flattened against her spine.

"I've got you." His voice was a low rumble against her ear, the contact between them almost a kiss before he stepped back and handed her the dress. "What I want is to keep you."

CHAPTER SEVEN

WITH HER HAIR AND MAKEUP already done, Connor had barely gotten his arms through the sleeves of his tuxedo shirt before Megan was stepping out of the master bath again. This time decked out in the metallic-silver bridesmaid dress that left nearly the full length of her toned legs on perfect display.

Damn.

Megan shifted under his scrutiny, smoothing her hands over her hips with downward strokes probably intended to eke out a few millimeters of additional coverage.

Not happening.

"I had nothing to do with picking out this dress."

As if he needed her to tell him. If Megan had been picking, he imagined she'd have selected something deceptively conservative. Like the dress she'd been wearing the night before. At first glance it had looked modest enough, but when he let his eyes linger for even a moment, the seductive hints had time to make an impact. The cut of the back, the line of the waist. The cling and fall, emphasizing all the right curves. Megan had an eye for what flattered her, but she managed it in a stylish, understated way. Something he liked.

Well, hell. He liked this dress too. But it was a different sort of appreciation happening here.

"Let me guess. Tina?" he asked, thinking it had to be she of the GOT SPERM T-shirt behind this kind of flash.

Megan smirked. "You'd think. But believe it or not, this was all Jodie. Something about the dress being a gift to us single girls."

"Bridesmaid's gift?"

"Jodie was convinced these dresses would give us the pick of the casino."

Connor let out a bark of laughter. "Well, she's got that right. And might I mention how utterly pleased I am you've decided to bring me along tonight. Especially considering the hard time I'd have had letting you out of my sight otherwise."

A wash of pink tinged Megan's cheeks as the smallest smile played at her lips. "Are you the jealous type?"

"Let's call it possessive." Her lids lifted, and seeing the pleasure in her eyes at his statement, he added, "But only when something is very important to me."

Pearly-white teeth pressed into Megan's lush little bottom lip as she turned away, fidgeting with the studs and links he'd set out on the polished mahogany dresser top. Her hair wound up the way it was, she couldn't hide the pretty color suffusing the skin along her neck and ears. And he couldn't fight the rush of pure masculine satisfaction at having driven it there.

After arranging everything into a neat row, Megan turned back to him. Her cheeks showing only the barest hint of her remaining blush. "I should get my shoes on. And you…"

She bent a little, reaching for the shoes set neatly at the wall. Stood, shifted and tried again. Pulled at the hem riding higher with each attempt.

Wow. Thank you, Jodie.

Flustered, Megan cleared her throat. Clearly working to maintain her poise.

"You should finish getting dressed yourself." She waved at his open shirt, her eyes lingering even as she turned her head. "We've got to get going pretty quickly."

"Mmm-hmm," he said again, making a mental note, once this better-than-a-late-night-cable-show was over and they left the villa, not to let Megan bend over for anything.

Catching on to his level of distraction, Megan shot him a

scathing glare…one that quickly dissolved into laughter. "This is ridiculous. Stop staring so I can get my shoes!"

Then, eyes to the ceiling, she muttered something adorably mild about men and Jodie and wishing she had a parka.

"Okay, low of me," he conceded, not even trying to make it believable. "I'm sorry."

"Right." She laughed, only, the sultry sound of it died on her lips as he stepped close, catching her hips in his hands, giving in to the temptation to flex his fingers…just once.

Megan's eyes went wide at the undeniably intimate contact, and he waited, gauging her response.

When she didn't push him away, he backed her toward the edge of the bed. "Why don't you sit, and I'll help you with the shoes."

Megan perched at the edge of the bed, still reeling from the feel of Connor's hands sliding over her hips, moving the fabric against her skin as he guided her to where he wanted her to be. She shouldn't have allowed it. Should have done more than stare up at him helplessly. But something inside her wouldn't react to Connor as a stranger.

Her body remembered him…even if her mind did not.

She wanted him. This sexy barefoot man, dressed in black tuxedo pants and a crisp, white shirt hanging dangerously open as he teased her. And for the first time, she understood the kind of mind-numbing allure that led women to make the worst decisions of their lives. And smile about it after.

Connor swept up her shoes with a finger through the straps and then knelt in front of her to lift her foot. "Do they hurt after all the walking last night?" he asked, running his thumb around her heel and then up through her arch.

She stared, too caught up in the intimacy of the scene and how shockingly good it felt to respond with more than the barest shake of her head.

"Good." Eyes locked with hers, he slipped the point of her shoe over her toes, gently fitting the heel and running a lazy circle around her ankle with his thumb. She watched, breathless, as his large hands deftly worked the delicate glass-beaded strap through its buckle.

So unbelievably sexy.

It was unreal.

It was…a fairy tale. Which was bad.

This man was telling her their marriage was based on the kind of up-front honesty and pragmatic realism that kept expectations attainable. And yet, everything about him—his incredible looks, his wealth, his knack for saying exactly what she needed to hear and, most of all, his romantic overtures—screamed *too good to be true.*

So what was she doing buying into the charade?

Letting herself see them years from now, chatting as they dressed together for some coming event.

Connor's finger slipped beneath the buckled strap. "Okay?"

"Perfect." Like everything else he'd shown her. Only, nothing and no one were actually perfect.

Connor's mouth pulled into a rueful slant. "You make *perfect* sound like it's not such a good thing. And like you aren't talking about your shoe."

But she was talking about the shoe, only not the way it fit.

"You're telling me this marriage between us is going to work because we aren't bringing any fairy-tale expectations into it. But here you are, down on one knee, fitting a glass slipper on my foot. Everything you do and say is like some fantasy come to life…which makes it hard to know what reality is actually going to feel like."

Connor gave her a thoughtful nod and set down her bejeweled foot. "I admit, I'm making every effort to sweep you off your feet. I want you to fall for me."

He picked up her other foot, giving it the same attention as the first. "But if it puts your mind to rest, I'm pretty sure Prince Charming wasn't using the old shoe excuse just to get his hands on his wife's leg."

Buckles complete, he let his hands skim up over her calves, stroking a light path behind her knees as he went on. "What's more, based on the target audience for those stories, I'd really hope he wasn't entertaining the kind of thoughts running through my mind as I watched you wrestling your short skirt. Because there was nothing PG about where my head was at."

"Really?"

A nod. "Strictly X stuff. I promise."

"Connor." His name was a plea on her lips, and the moment it sounded, the humor in his eyes faded and the lines of his face hardened.

"We're good together, Megan. It's not about glass slippers or fairy tales or love at any sight. It's not about private schools or mutual goals or any of the other things we've talked about today. It's about you and me fitting together. It's about this feeling of rightness you told me about last night. The one I've had since I met you. And I keep seeing signs of it today. Tell me. Tell me you feel it too."

"I feel it." The connection was there. Undeniable between them.

But whether *feeling* right together for one day was the same as actually *being* right together through the rest of their lives…

"I just don't know—" The words died in her throat at the sight of the burning heat staring down at her. The desire blazing in his eyes. Desire for her.

The same desire firing through her body, spilling hot through her center and filling her mind with a smoky haze. Suddenly she wanted those big hands everywhere on her. She didn't want to worry about good judgment or long-term consequences. She simply wanted this man, whose promises sounded too good to be true, to deliver on the one in his eyes.

"Connor," she whispered, drawing her leg slowly in, and the man with it. "You make me want…"

God, she couldn't say it. Couldn't even think it. All her rational thought was tangled up in the rising awareness between them, the slow glide of his touch over her skin, the need simmering between them.

And then he was off the floor, one hand moving from her leg to brace on the mattress beside her hip. The other climbing to the outside of her shoulder, so all she could do was lie back, staring into his eyes as his large body moved over her own. His knee replaced his left hand at her hip, and she was surrounded.

He was so close she could feel the heat radiating off his body, the wash of his breath against her jaw, the tickle of his open shirt grazing her arms. Decadent. Intimate. Too seductive to resist. Her fingers closed around the draping fabric, pulling him toward her until only the barest space remained.

She pulled again. A subtle nudge. Then a stronger tug, but all it earned her was another one of those devastating half smiles and the slow shake of Connor's head as he reached into his pocket and withdrew her ring.

Braced on one arm and his knees above her, Connor slid his free hand up her left arm, rolling the glinting diamond band along the path of her skin until he held it poised above the tip of her ring finger, so close she could feel an almost magnetic pull from the wanting.

It would be so easy to give in. Give him what he wanted. What, on some level, she wanted too.

Let him slide that platinum band over her finger, and say yes to what would inevitably feel good in the moment, but had the potential to devastate if she wasn't careful.

Forcing the air in her lungs to move again, she managed a single word. "Wait."

Connor's smile quirked suggestively. "Nervous? I promise I'll be gentle. I've done this before."

Her eyes closed as she once again found herself relieved by his sense of humor and ability to lighten the mood without undermining the seriousness of what was at stake.

Finding more breath, she whispered, "We can't. Not yet."

"Why not? We're already married." His voice dropped lower as he lightly teased the diamond band around the tip of her finger. "I can tell you want it."

Yes, right then, she did. But wearing his ring meant giving up her plans. Giving up the security of a future she could control completely. Giving up a promise she'd made to herself... for the chance of something so much more.

Connor was poised above her, his sharp gaze studying her every minuscule reaction. Hesitation. Blink, blush and tremor.

Tentatively, she placed her free hand against the center of his chest. His bare skin was shades darker than her own. Hot. Firm. Tempting her toward reckless action just to ensure she had more time to enjoy it.

But that simply wasn't who she was. If he knew her at all, he would understand.

"I'm not ready. I'm not sure I can give you what you're asking for."

A nod. Then, "Wear it anyway. You're still my wife for now. Why not try the whole package on for size and see how it feels?"

Her gaze drifted over to the band of diamonds so close to sliding home. Each flawless stone throwing off light in all directions. It was exquisite.

Nothing could compete with this ring.

Swallowing once, she peered back up at Connor, who waited above her, the possessive intent in his eyes making her ache to give in. But she couldn't do it.

"It's probably better if I don't." Trying to match his lighter tone, she curled her fingers into her palm and dodged, "And about this whole being-married thing. I was thinking we might not mention it. Let everyone think I'm just a cheap floozy rather than the honest woman you've made me."

CHAPTER EIGHT

CONNOR SWALLOWED, his body going still. "You don't want them to know."

Guileless eyes met his. "I'd prefer they don't."

And then she was wiggling out from beneath him. Crawling off the bed from one side as he backed off from the other, returning the ring to his pocket.

Megan stood in front of the bureau mirror frowning at the few hairs out of place from their brief roll in the sack. They had to leave soon, and considering he'd actually hired someone in to sculpt her hair into perfection, it made sense she'd be trying to fix her look.

But suddenly all he could see was a woman concerned with her image, and for the first time he wondered if he didn't really know her after all.

He shook his head. It couldn't be right.

"I thought you didn't lie."

It was the quality in her he appreciated above all others. It was *important* to him.

One brow shot high as she turned to meet his eyes. "I don't. But that doesn't mean I walk around regurgitating every personal detail of my existence without prompt. I'd prefer you not bring it up, because seriously, no one is going to ask."

A lie of omission. Well, that was irony.

He knew all about them. Had been one for the first decade of his life and had sworn never to be one again. And yet here he was, married to a woman making a dirty little secret of him from the start.

Freud would have a field day with this.

Okay, so it wasn't as though he'd discovered Megan stowing the ring in her car's ashtray while she hit the bars. They'd been married for less than twenty-four hours, and she wasn't even certain she wanted to wait another twenty-four before filing for divorce. But still, her not wanting people to know rubbed him in all the wrong places. Partly because one of the first things to attract him about her was the way she owned her life. Her actions. She wasn't making excuses or apologies or even taking the easy way out of an explanation. In the few hours he'd known her before he talked her into changing the plan for both their lives, she'd made him believe in who she was. How she lived. And this—this secret didn't fit with that.

Which made him wonder about some of the other things he'd believed.

"I told you honesty was important to me. We talked about it *today*." And same as last night, she'd agreed about the critical importance of trust in any marriage, but especially one not based on love.

"Connor..." Megan's voice had taken a stern edge, as though she was the one who didn't like what was being said. "This is my cousin, and while we aren't spectacularly close, if I show up with your ring on, no one is going to pay attention to Gail's wedding at all. It wouldn't be fair to her. I'm sorry, but I hope you can respect my feelings."

Connor's head snapped up, the lead boulder in his gut evaporating under her words.

"You aren't trying to hide something you're embarrassed about?"

Her head tilted slightly, as if she wasn't quite sure what she was hearing. "You mean because you're such an unattractive, insufferable dog who's probably going to fleece me for everything I'm worth...and I wasn't smart enough to chew my arm off for a clean escape?"

The laughter was back, bolstered by more relief than he'd thought he could experience. "Something like that."

Megan gave a tiny smile before turning thoughtful. Then, "I suppose, if I'm being totally honest, I am a little embarrassed about it. I mean, I made one of the biggest decisions of my life during a night when I'd drunk so much I don't even remember doing it. But I'm not under any delusions about keeping our marriage under wraps. Everyone at this wedding is going to know about us—approximately two seconds after I talk to my mother. Which is why I haven't called her yet."

"What if we decide to divorce? You could sweep it under the rug."

Megan laughed. "Maybe you could, but not me. Even knowing she can't keep a confidence to save her life, I don't keep secrets from my mother. I'll tell her what's happened as soon as I get home. And then the minute I hang up…" Megan's eyes closed, and she drew in a slow breath. "Believe me. I'll be hearing about this for the rest of my life. Regardless of the outcome."

Connor offered a hand to Megan. "You okay with that?"

Megan wagged her head a little, eyes on the ceiling. "It's my life. So yes. I'm good with it."

Damn, he liked the things that came out of this woman's mouth. He liked the way she thought. The way she cared. The way she lived. The way she stood by the choices she believed in. And despite his initial reaction to her not wearing his ring, he liked the way she could see past her own situation to consider the feelings of those around her.

That strength of character was what he wanted for his family.

"And with me?" he asked. "If I promise not to bring up the wedding, are you still good with me?"

Megan's eyes were soft, steady as she met his. "I'm good with you too."

The wedding went off without a hitch. Gail and Roy tied the knot in a chapel not so different, according to Connor, from the one where they'd been married the night before. The vows were made, the rings exchanged and then the marriage was sealed with a kiss. It was beautiful, despite Jodie and Tina making jokes at Megan's expense throughout the ceremony, laughingly suggesting in her lack of experience she'd managed to botch her one-night stand by dragging it into the next day.

She'd been prepared for the barrage of teasing. Had warned Connor about it. But what she hadn't expected was how protective her new husband was. And the way he managed to sabotage most every joke the quibbling duo attempted. Still, the girls were nothing if not persistent.

"So, really, Connor, what are you doing here?" Jodie asked, straining to be heard over the nightclub music booming around them. "I mean, sure, Megan reeled you in last night, but aren't you ready to rip the hook out and take off yet?"

Whether she'd been going for flirtation or just a joke, the question was typically tactless, and Megan reminded herself white-chocolate martinis weren't a solution. Not since the idea of them alone had her stomach ready to revolt.

Connor stretched his arm across the back of Megan's chair, the warmth of it permeating the tuxedo jacket he'd wrapped her up in as soon as the ceremony ended. "Not at all. Megan's incredible and I see this relationship going the distance."

Tina leaned forward, putting her best assets on display. "Relationship?"

A slow heat began to build in Megan's cheeks as all eyes shifted to where Connor's thumb ran a lazy pattern against her shoulder. He'd been attentive without being overly demonstrative throughout the evening, obviously making an effort to respect her wishes and keep their marriage under wraps at least until the ink dried on Gail's matching certificate. But this line of questioning could lead them toward the truth in a hurry if something didn't change.

Tina's shrewd eyes darted between them twice, before she stepped back with a cool laugh. "Oh, Megan, tell me you didn't?"

Her heart sank. Somehow Tina had figured it out. Gail, who was waiting as expectantly as everyone else, would never forgive her.

"Tell me you didn't go and make another *friend*?" The last word fell with such disgust it took Megan a second to realize she hadn't been discovered. She didn't need to feel ashamed for hijacking her cousin's wedding. Relief washed over her in a wave, buoying her mood enough she couldn't contain the smile stretching across her face.

"What are you talking about?" Connor asked, casually enough. Only, something about his voice sounded off, and as she turned to face him, she didn't like the look of his half smile at all.

"Nothing. It's nothing, Connor," she said, hoping he'd recognize the plea in her eyes for him to leave it. The plea and the promise that she'd explain later when they weren't within glowering distance of Gail's wedding party. "I'd love another tonic. Any chance you'd come to the bar with me?"

After a beat, the smile turned more genuine and Connor stood, offering her his hand. "How about a dance first."

Before she could mutter a protest, he had her flush against his chest and was deftly leading her with his hands, thighs, chest and hips into the midst of the clubgoers. Moving in a way that was all easy rhythm and physical confidence. Nothing *friendly* about it.

Within a few minutes, she'd returned to the state that teetered between laughter and lust and was totally unique to her experience with Connor, leaving Tina and Jodie and all their barbs a distant memory.

Connor signed off on the open-bar bill for their group and then grabbed the tall tonic and ice Megan had requested, eyeing their table like a man about to face the gallows. Megan was still in the ladies' room, but something told him waiting for her outside the door would smack of stalker. So rather, he made his way to the table prepared to deflect the pointed questions about his bank accounts, Reed Industries' worth and whether Megan had managed to snag any of his sperm.

He was ready to get out of there. First, because his wife's laugh, which was all kinds of sexy abandon, was proving to be a temptation he couldn't resist much longer, and second, because Tina and Jodie, and even Gail, were grating hard. Pushing buttons he hadn't known he had. Megan's ability to let it roll off her back gave him the sense she'd had too much practice. And he didn't like it.

As it turned out, Gail had kicked off her shoes and propped her feet on one vacant chair, leaving the only other available between Tina and Jodie, whose antics had vacillated between mildly annoying and downright nasty.

No, thanks.

Roy and his two groomsmen were huddled in the same kind of quiet conversation they'd been engaged in through the rest of the evening—excepting the ceremony, of course—the monosyllabic, extended-silence kind.

Opting to stand off at the side, he watched the dance floor while he waited for Megan.

A cackle of laughter had the muscles of his spine tightening unpleasantly. And then Gail's chiding reprimand. "You two are terrible!"

He didn't want to know. Shouldn't even have been able to hear over the music.

A less-than-delicate snort from Tina. "Please, it's pathetic."

But their voices.

And Jodie. "She can't stop collecting these guys."

That brought his head around. They hadn't noticed him standing behind them, and again they were talking about his wife. The woman who'd fought with him in an effort to respect this day.

"I don't know who she thinks she's kidding with this one. There's no way—"

"No way," chimed in Tina.

"—he's anything more than the next 'friend,' trying to do her some sort of favor. Keep us off her back probably."

Gail held up a hand between them. Good. Her cousin, showing some loyalty. Only, then she started talking and his vision went red.

* * *

Megan's steps faltered as she approached the table.

"…keep wondering with all these 'buddies' is if she's *so great to talk with*, then what exactly is *bad enough* to drive these guys away?"

Megan's breath caught in her throat as Gail sloppily speculated on her life with Connor standing directly behind her.

He'd heard.

She knew by his utter lack of reaction. The stillness in a form that was so much energy.

Jodie nodded sagely as Tina glanced up and, catching Megan's eyes, let out a snort of laughter.

Closing her eyes, she drew several deep breaths.

They'd already put in their time. They could leave.

Maybe he wouldn't say anything and they could just forget it.

When Megan opened her eyes, Connor was already around the table, no doubt as ready to make a break for it as she was. More. Gail wasn't even his relative.

Or…well, not by blood anyway. Lucky.

And then he was at her side, sliding a hand around her waist as he pulled her close. Closer. And closer still until her eyes went wide as his marauding hand slid across her bottom in a slow, blatant caress to rest at the very top of her thigh. Face burrowed into the side of her neck, he drew a long breath, teasing his nose along the sensitive stretch of skin behind her ear.

He was making a point. Letting them see what she'd asked him to rein in for the sake of Gail's special day. Really, she couldn't hold it against him. In fact, it sort of made him her own personal hero.

Letting her pull back enough for decency, Connor smiled down at her. "What do you think about wrapping it up here?"

Tina's chin pulled back and Jodie rolled her eyes. Gail scrunched up her nose and stuck out her bottom lip. "No. You've got to stay. Bride's prerogative and all. It's my day, so park it."

Connor's menacing half smile slanted over his lips as he looked at the table. All nonchalance, with one hand still resting dangerously low on her hip, the other tucked casually in his pocket.

"Bride's prerogative," he murmured. "Definitely."

She should have seen it coming, should have known. But it wasn't until he'd caught her hand that she saw what he was holding.

The floor dropped out from under her.

"Megan," he said with a doting smile and a steely glint in his eyes. "I know you wanted to wait to announce our news, but I honestly can't. Not. Another. Second."

She was too stunned to react when he slid that gorgeous glittering band over her finger, raising their joined hands for everyone to see. "I know it was fast, but there wasn't a chance in hell I was letting this woman get away."

Gail was the first one to pick her jaw up off the floor, her watery eyes now darting between the ring she wore and Megan's. "You got married," she gasped. "At my wedding?"

Megan started fumbling for something to say, for an apology maybe, though it didn't really seem right. She opened her mouth, only to have the air squeezed out of her lungs by Connor's arms wrapping snug around her. "No, of course not," he assured with all the sensitivity of an assassin. "We got married first. This morning."

Tina and Jodie were both shaking their heads as if understanding was impossible.

"I know it's early, but I think we've waited long enough to get back to our honeymoon. So if you'll excuse us…" And with everyone watching, Megan found herself swept off her feet, tucked into Connor's arms. "Drinks are on me tonight. Congratulations."

CHAPTER NINE

"WHAT IN THE HELL do you think you're doing?" Megan demanded from the far side of the elevator where she stood, hands on hips, eyes boring into him like little embers of hell.

Connor snapped the picture from his phone then slipped the device back into his tux pocket before it ended up incinerated beneath his wife's fiery glare, or more likely crushed beneath the spike of her sexy glass slipper.

"Documenting our first fight."

For a moment, all the red-hot rage directed his way turned to utter shock, leaving her sputtering in a way he couldn't deny he was getting a serious kick out of. But in a blink, she rocketed back to fury, leaning into the space between them, her voice going lethally low. "I can't *believe* you did that."

"Come on, it's something for the scrapbook. You'll thank me later."

"You know good and well I'm not talking about a picture."

Yeah, he did. The way he knew taking a snap of her when she was this cranked up was probably a move just short of suicide, but like his decision to break his promise to her back in the club, it was one he wouldn't regret.

"We had a deal," she hissed, her eyes darting between him and the elevator's digital display. "But maybe you forgot. Or perhaps our agreement didn't suit your needs at the time, so you *just changed your mind*."

The car slowed, sounding a low chime to alert them they'd arrived at their floor. The doors soundlessly opened and Megan turned forward—her face a mask of calm, belied only by the rapid pulse at her neck. Placing his hand at the small of her back, they stepped out into the main floor.

"Definitely the latter," he answered quietly at her ear.

A taunt, almost daring her to lose her cool in the midst of all these people. But not Megan. She kept it together, impressing him more and more. Confirming once again how well suited she was to being his wife. Not that he'd make a habit of goading her in public or out of it. He didn't expect much fighting, but it was important to know how she would handle it.

From there, they walked silently through the hotel, before arriving at their private villa.

He was more than ready to go toe-to-toe with her on this point, regardless of what kind of mad she had on. That scene at the nightclub was beyond unacceptable.

The second they were inside, Megan spun on him. *"You promised me."*

He had. But circumstances weren't what he'd expected, requiring a judgment call, and he'd made one. Firming up his stance, he crossed his arms.

"Did you hear what they said?" he demanded, giving his own mad its head. "I wasn't going to let those catty, backbiting—"

Her hand cut through the air. "I don't care what they said. All that matters to me is what *you* said. *Your* word. What it's worth. What I can believe."

He held her stare, not backing down. *"You can believe* I took you to be my wife. To honor, respect and *protect*, for all the days of our life."

Megan blinked up at him, suddenly at a loss for words. "Those were our vows?"

"They were mine. And I meant them. I'm not the kind of husband to twiddle my thumbs while my wife is maligned. I would have liked to accommodate you tonight, Megan. I fully intended to. But in a choice between breaking my vow to protect my wife and breaking my vow to protect your cousin's 'special day,' you can bet I'll be putting you first every time."

"Oh." She swallowed past the knot of emotion in her throat, trying to force it back down. Trying not to allow a few simple words the power to leave her vulnerable.

Then after a moment, Connor closed the distance between them, pulling her into his chest. "I'm sorry I had to break my promise to you. But I meant what I said about taking care of you. I won't stand by while someone hurts you."

"I could have handled it." She'd been doing it her whole life.

"Why should you?"

"Gail deserved to have her wedding day." And more than that, because he'd agreed to let her!

"Yes, but so did you." Connor caught her face in his hands, tipping it back so she was looking up at him. "Just because you don't remember doesn't mean it doesn't count."

Everything he said sounded so right. Tempted her to trust. To leap. But the void she was looking out over was simply too great to ignore.

Searching his eyes, she asked the question that was the crux of her fears and reluctance. "What if you change your mind?"

"That's the point, Megan. I won't.

"Commitment—" he rubbed the bridge of his nose as he let out a thoughtful sigh "—it's very important to me. I'm not looking to fill some temporary position, Megan. I want a wife who will stand by me for the duration." Only, then something in his expression shifted. His eyes went distant for a beat before snapping back to hers. Sharper. More intense. "Maybe if you had more time…"

"You mean date?" she asked, knowing she wouldn't go along with it. No more waiting around to see whether something panned out. No more false hopes and years of indecision—

"No," he said with a hard shake of his head, confirming they were in agreement on the no dating. Connor leaned into her space, putting his face before hers so the sincerity in his eyes was front and center. "Understand this, Megan. You're my wife and I want to keep it that way. But I realize everything hasn't fallen into place for you the way it did last night and I'm asking for a big leap. Still, I'm confident, with a little time, it will.

So I propose a trial period. Give me three months. If you don't think we suit, I give you a divorce and you return to the life you had planned. In the meantime, we start as we mean to go on. You live with me…as my wife."

Her throat felt dry, her heart pounding too fast.

It was crazy. What he was suggesting… "You'd introduce me to your friends and business associates? What if I wasn't happy and wanted to leave?"

"You go. Megan, I'm asking you to give our marriage a shot, not to lock yourself in some prison you can't get out of. Granted, I don't believe you'd leave without giving us a chance. Not once you'd made a commitment—one you remember making, that is. Besides, you're not going to want to leave."

He made it sound so simple. She'd been so tempted, time and again throughout the day—but the doubts. They simply weighed too much.

"I've finally found a way to be happy, Connor. I know you think because love isn't a factor that this arrangement you're suggesting comes without risk, but it doesn't. Not for me. I can't put my faith in someone else again. And that's what you're asking me to do. It—it hurts too much to be let down. I'm sorry."

"You don't think the reward would be worth the risk?"

"I don't know. And maybe that in itself should tell us both something," she whispered.

"Yeah, it does. It tells me instead of waiting, hoping you'd remember or come around, expecting you to see the big picture when I hadn't given you all of the pieces, I should have done this."

And before she could blink, he'd pulled her into a kiss.

Megan was flush to his body. Her hands trapped between them, where they'd come up in a stunted defense that stopped before it really began—stopped at the strange familiarity of this intimacy she couldn't quite remember—stopped at the foreign heat inexplicably swirling like a whirlpool through her center, pulling deeper, concentrating with every back-and-forth pass of his mouth over hers.

No wonder she'd blocked it out.

Connor's kiss was even better than she'd imagined. So good, she felt the resistant determination slipping from her body even as she grasped after it. But it was gone, having taken the edge of aggression in the dark depths of Connor's eyes with it. The hands at her shoulders snaked around her waist and into her hair. The pressure against her lips increased and she opened to him.

Afraid to miss even a second, she couldn't blink and her eyes remained locked with his, anticipating the taste and texture of him mixed with her own.

Only, rather than take his fill, Connor barely breached her mouth, skimming the inner swell of her bottom lip with a slow, agonizing lick so compelling it temporarily overwhelmed even the instinct to breathe.

Using the hand wound loose in her hair to angle her head, he deepened the kiss. Enticing her into a return of action—the tentative flick of her tongue against his.

It was all the invitation he needed, and hands tightening at her hip and hair, Connor's low growl of satisfaction slipped through her lips an instant before the firm thrust and retreat of his tongue. The penetrating claim wringing a response too strong, too immediate, too intense to deny. And then she was clutching at him, pressing close even as he pulled her closer still.

It wasn't enough.

Not for either of them.

Connor grasped her bottom in a firm, kneading caress. Then the back of her thigh, pulling it up along the outside of his leg. Rocking into her so she felt the steely length of him against her belly and the hard press of solid muscle between her legs.

From somewhere in the back of her mind, she was vaguely aware of all the reasons this was such a bad idea...only, she didn't care.

Couldn't stop.

Another deep thrust, and then Connor's devouring mouth moved down to her jaw, her neck. Licking, sucking, pulling at the tender spot until she'd thrown her head back, and her hands restlessly worked between them, grasping at the panels of his shirt. Trying to get a hold enough to rip it open.

"Megan, Megan," he groaned, the hot wash of his breath as intoxicating as the friction of his lips. "Baby, it's going to be so good. Tell me you want this."

"Yes," she moaned. "Yes, yes, yes, please. I want you."

His knee pressed higher between her legs, raising her skirt as he rocked the thick slab of his thigh against her intimate flesh in a way that had tendrils of pleasure sliding through her center.

Flicking a teasing lick over the corner of her mouth, he murmured, "Tell me, yes...tell me you'll be my wife."

This wasn't the time for that discussion. This wasn't the time for talking at all. "Later. Please, we'll talk more about it later."

His hips dipped lower, giving her a fleeting taste of the thick ridge of his erection.

Once.

Oh, God...so hot.

Twice.

Her fingers knotted in his hair as liquid heat spilled through her belly.

And then again.

Her breath rushed out on a gasp at the sharp, needy spasm deep within her.

"Tell me you're coming home with me tomorrow."

"Connor, please," she begged, her body on fire.

"You don't even know how much I like the sound of that," he whispered against her parted lips. "How much I want to hear it against my ear as I move inside you...pushing in deep..."

A whimper escaped her at the erotic images sliding through her with the rough stroke of his voice.

"...taking you higher and higher...until you shatter in my arms."

"Yes..." She was about to shatter already.

"Yes, what, Megan?" he asked, trailing his fingertips from the back of her knee to the curve of her bottom and back. "You know what I want to hear."

CHAPTER TEN

WAIT. WHAT? "Are you…blackmailing me with…sex?"

"I don't know." His hips pulled back a fraction of an inch. "Would it work?"

It would.

Even knowing the game he played, Megan was a hairbreadth from promising anything Connor asked for—if it meant he'd finish what he started.

Only, somehow in the past seconds, her stalled-out mind had sputtered to life again. Weakly turning over the events unfolding around her. Events that would shape the rest of her life.

"No," she choked out, forcing her hands to be still. Her eyes to open and meet the burning black of Connor's stare.

"Damn."

She could see the indecision in his eyes…the debate whether to try again. Try harder.

A tremor of hope slipped through her belly at the thought. One she ruthlessly pushed aside.

"What is this?" she asked, waving a hand between them.

He shook his head, an almost bewildered look on his cocky face. "It's hot."

It was more than hot. "It's distracting. I can't think."

"Good, agree to give me three months."

But before she could even contemplate giving him three minutes, his mouth was over hers again, his tongue sliding between her lips in slow, seductive thrusts. Once again tempting her reservations to abandon their posts.

Heart racing, breath ragged, she shook her head, forcing her hands to center at Connor's chest and then giving him a small push. She couldn't agree to anything. Whatever state she'd been in last night, at this moment, the impairment of her judgment was at record level.

"Megan," he murmured, watching her from beneath heavy lids.

Oh, hell, that look. She swallowed, taking a step back. And then another. She needed to get away. Needed space to breathe. To think.

"Come on, baby. Don't run away. Let's sit on the couch and talk."

Her gaze shot to the couch. Within a blink, it had become fodder for more scenarios than her experience could justify— a den of seduction, rife with erotic potential.

She *had* been reading a lot lately.

"I'll keep my hands to myself," came another low, rumbling assurance, pulling her focus back to Connor. Standing where she'd left him, the shirt she'd been trying to free him of spread wide to reveal the hard muscles banding his abdomen and the perfect discs of his nipples.

Her mouth watered as another couchside scenario accosted her.

"Sure you will." Fine, maybe he would. Maybe it wasn't *his hands* she was worried about.

"Don't believe me? You could always tie my hands." Connor grasped one end of the tie hanging loose at his open neck, let it twist around his finger as he held it out in offering. His wicked smile pushing new limits. "Unless you'd prefer—"

"No!" Okay, it definitely wasn't his hands she was worried about. And with what she was thinking, she wasn't sure she'd ever be able to sit on any couch again, let alone that one.

She forced her feet to move one after the other until she'd cleared the stairs and made the master suite again. Arms crossed, she gripped the hem of her dress and pulled it over her head. Stepped into the shower and jerked the tap to cold, bracing for the crush of clarity she prayed the icy deluge would bring.

"Agghgh!" she half shrieked as arctic needles fired against her overheated skin, coating her body with the cold wash of reason returned.

She'd been about to agree to…anything.

Marriage.

Moving across the country.

And God help her, even with the chill of reality raining down over her…all she could think about was the way his kiss had all but consumed her.

A low groan of reluctant need slipped past her lips, and she positioned her face beneath the pounding spray, waiting for the cold to beat its way through her thick skull and to snuff the smoky thoughts in her mind and the fire blazing through her veins.

"Damn, Megan. I like it when you make those sounds."

The lock. She hadn't even thought about it.

Blinking the running water from her face, she turned to look out the clear glass of the shower stall to see Connor leaning against the wall across the room. His half smile was at full strength, seductive and hungry.

"What are you doing in there, sweetheart?"

"Trying to clear my head."

One brow arched and he pushed off the wall, his predatory gaze sliding over her body.

Why wasn't she embarrassed by his obvious perusal? Not that there was anywhere to hide. The clear glass was more a display case than any kind of shelter from searching eyes. And yet, his eyes on her felt natural. Easy.

Not at all the way she'd felt with other men, but then, she'd been working outside the norm from the word go that morning. She should stop making the comparisons.

"Hmm. Clarity looks good on you. Maybe I could use some too."

This time it was Megan's mouth that tipped. *Definitely.* This guy needed to have the fire inside him doused. "You think?"

Connor's hands were on his half-open fly, finishing the job she'd started down in the entryway. And then he was stepping out of his tuxedo pants, leaving them in a heap on the floor as he took a step toward the shower.

Megan's mouth dropped open as she realized just exactly what she'd been inviting.

Was her brain ever going to work right again?

His hands moved to the black boxer briefs straining atop the force of his erection. Those went next, and then he was completely, mouthwateringly naked. His body more beautiful than her fantasies could have imagined. And he was closing the distance between them. Coming for her. Opening the glass door, his eyes blazing hot enough to make her body burn even under—

"What the—?" he barked out as he hopped into the far corner of the shower.

Megan knew she probably shouldn't have laughed, but there was something decidedly satisfying in, for once, not being the one caught off guard. And the stunned confusion etched across the frozen mask of Connor's face was simply too irresistible.

The rapidly thawing mask of confusion.

"You did that on purpose," he charged, maintaining his position beyond the stream of water.

"You said you wanted the clarity," she answered, her body going alert as his focus narrowed on her breasts and then lower. They were both naked. Standing at opposite ends of the oversize stall. The second Connor grabbed for her, she darted out the door, laughing. "Who was I to stop you?"

A deep growl sounded behind her as she reached for the plush warmth of the robe folded over the lip of the tub. Wrapping up, she turned back to the shower and froze. Hands flat against the wall above the tap, muscles flexed and straining, Connor, braced beneath the spray as the cold beat over his body. Then with a shake of his head, he focused on her where she stood beyond the glass.

"I'll be honest, this doesn't work as well as I'd expected it to."

"My thoughts exactly," she answered, half mesmerized by the picture before her.

"Megan, I'm trying really hard to stay where I am right now, but if you don't walk out that door, I'm going to walk out this one and put you against it."

Her mouth fell open.

First the couch. Now the door. It was as if he had seductive superpowers with his ability to infuse the most mundane household objects with deviant potential.

"Or maybe that's what you're waiting for." The promise in his voice was what had her feet moving past the threshold, where she dared one glance back at Connor, who stood watching her, his expression dark, smile wiped clean from his face.

Connor's palm hit the tile with a wet smack as he swore under his breath.

Tempted as she was, she wouldn't take the risk.

Grabbing the soap, he scoured his body with rough strokes, using the task to give himself the time he needed to work through his options.

But damn it, none of them were going to give him what he wanted. Megan coming home with him.

Sure, he was fairly certain, even though it went against her general morals, if he offered Megan no strings, he'd have her beneath him before the water dried from his body. But he didn't want a single night with her. And he wasn't after the dog-and-pony show of dating either. Even with someone like Megan, he didn't want to sink another year into a relationship lacking the authenticity of people who knew they were in it for more than a three- or four-hour window at a stretch. He didn't want to see her at her best. Primped and prepared for some night of romance. He didn't want to be waiting for the *real* to start.

He wanted the *real* right now.

And he'd had it. Until it spilled through his fingers like an overturned cocktail.

Now, no matter how he tried to show her what it had been like, tell her what he'd learned, make her feel the insanity of the connection between them…it wasn't the same. Wasn't enough.

She was going to fly away tomorrow. And nothing he did was going to stop her.

Jerking the tap off, he rubbed the water from his eyes and shook out his hair.

Then, wrapping a towel around his hips, he readied himself for the goodbye he was certain awaited on the other side of the door. Or more likely down in the living room. But definitely not on the couch.

Enough pussyfooting around.

He swung open the bathroom door, determined to face the music like a man—and rooted to his spot, stunned by the sight of Megan, swimming in her giant robe, feet tucked beneath her in the wingback at the far corner of the master suite.

"Okay," she said, nervously wringing her hands. "I'll be your wife."

Megan was talking, but damned if he'd understood a word she said after *I'll be your wife.* In a heartbeat he'd crossed the room and had her in his arms. Her mouth was still moving when his crushed down, silencing the words he hadn't been able to follow. She could tell him later, when the adrenaline rush deafening him to everything but the roar of victory quieted inside his head. Until then, he'd keep her mouth busy with something more productive than talk.

Hands splayed over his chest, she pulled back from him, laughing even as he tried to follow her retreat. "Wait," she pleaded, her hands moving from his chest to frame his jaw. "Wait, Connor. We need to get a few things straight before we go any further."

Walking them back to the bed, he shook his head. "Later. Postnuptial agreement, whatever, we'll work it out. Tomorrow."

"No, that's not what—" Then, twisting her head around, she looked behind her. "No, Connor. I'm serious. Not the bed—"

Only, he was already tipping Megan back onto it. "I know you liked the door idea, but give the bed a chance. You won't be disappointed."

And then his mouth was on hers again, his hand following the smooth line of her thigh to her bare hip. And hell, yes, she was arching into him, moaning around the thrust of his tongue, clutching at his shoulders and then his hair. Opening wider to him and following the retreat of his tongue with the light flick of her own.

She was so sexy. She was *his*.

And he was going to taste every…single…inch of her tonight.

His mouth was on her neck, his tongue sliding over the rapid beat of her pulse when Megan's muffled curse, followed by an urgent wriggle and squirm, had him pulling back to meet her eyes.

"Damn it."

Her face screwed up into a knot of acute frustration, making Connor pull back even more as, baffled, he watched her scoot from the bed.

"*Now*, Connor. We need to talk now. Because I can't agree to everything. We need some ground rules."

"Ground rules." He didn't like the sound of that. "Such as?"

Tightening the belt on her robe, she shifted her weight and squinted at him. "No sex."

Connor's teeth ground down as he drew a long breath through his nose. "You mean…tonight?"

But even as he asked, he knew the answer.

"No. I'm talking about at all. Through the three trial months."

Forcing himself to laugh instead of swear, he shook his head. "Forget it, Megan. This is a real marriage we're trying on, and sex is a healthy, normal part of it."

"It's too distracting," she protested. "I couldn't even think straight when you and I were—" her hand waved back and forth through the air between them "—on the bed. And I'm talking about changing the plans for the rest of my life. I *need* to be able to think."

His brow furrowed. "You'll have plenty of time to think, sweetheart. How about I promise not to 'distract' you when we're discussing something important?"

"Yeah, I'm not sure your concession is going to be enough. When we're together…even kissing…Connor, I can't think enough to tell you to stop when my future is on the line."

Okay, grinning like a fool probably wasn't sending the best

message, but damn, he liked what he was hearing. "You seemed to manage it pretty well…and more than once."

"Barely!"

"Have I mentioned how happy I am you married me?"

"Connor, I'm serious—"

"I'm serious too," he said, following her off the bed and taking her shoulders in his hands. "As far as getting pregnant goes, obviously we'll wait until you're confident this is the life you want. But sex? Not a chance. I'm going to seduce you, Megan."

"I'll say no," she whispered, her eyes already drifting to his mouth.

"Fair warning—" his thumb moved to the pale pink line where her bottom lip became skin "—if you do, I'll stop."

She nodded, closing her eyes when the motion caused him to stroke across that bit of sensitive flesh. So pretty.

"I know you will."

Her eyes opened, and this time she looked him over from damp head to precariously situated towel to toe and back again, as though steeling herself against temptation.

This was his wife!

The muscles in her throat moved up and down as she swallowed. Twice. Then those gorgeous blue pools blinked up at him, determination doing its downright best to put in a showing.

"I can resist you."

Connor gave in to the slow grin pushing at his lips. "You can try."

CHAPTER ELEVEN

"ARE YOU OUT OF YOUR ever-loving mind?" Jeff demanded, his outrage reaching through the phone as clearly as if the man himself had crawled through the line to grab him and shake.

"Would you believe out of my mind, over the moon and totally in love?" Connor asked, shouldering his carry-on as he left the airport newsstand.

"No" was Jeff's flat, less-than-amused reply.

"Yeah, well, you're right." Sidestepping a couple locked in a passionate embrace, he scanned the gates and checked his watch. "I'm perfectly sane. Grounded, with my feet planted firmly in reality, and married to a gorgeous, sexy, intelligent woman who happens to be everything I'm looking for in a wife."

"Wow, I didn't realize you were looking for a gold-digging brainwasher, Connor, or I'd have pointed out the throngs of them throwing themselves at your feet for the last decade. What the hell happened, man. Did she drug you?"

Connor's jaw tightened, his teeth grinding down.

He'd known what people would think. The conclusions they'd draw. And he'd told himself he didn't care. That neither of them would. Hell, Megan wasn't afraid to fly in the face of convention any more than he was. But just as at the wedding, that protective instinct had him ready to throw down over those disparaging comments.

"Not even close. In fact, I suppose the case could be made *I* actually drugged *her.*"

There she was. Back from the coffee bar, a tray loaded with

a couple of roadies and a pastry bag in one hand, a laptop back-pack hanging from the other. He slowed his steps, preferring to get this cleared up out of earshot.

"Um…Connor, what are you talking about?"

"I let her drink too much and she ended up blacking out most of the night."

"Let me guess," came Jeff's dry reply. "She remembered the part about getting married, though."

"Yeah, but unfortunately she didn't remember *why* she'd thought it was such a great idea at the time. Took some effort on my part to remind her. Even now, she's still on the fence, but she's willing to give it a chance. We're on our way to Denver to pack her things."

"You're serious?"

He wasn't sure he'd ever heard Jeff's voice squeak that way, and the sound of it pushed the smile he'd started this call with back to his lips.

"As a heart attack. You'll have to take my word for it, but, Jeff, I *know* her. And I *like* her a hell of a lot."

Then because he simply couldn't pass on the opportunity to goad an old friend when the opportunity was right there, he added, "Back on the horse, like you said."

"Speaking of… Does she know about Caro?"

"She does. I told her the first night." He cleared his throat and looked out over the tarmac. "Then again yesterday." He'd been damn lucky she'd asked him about any serious relation-ships during their refresher course in *Know Thy Mate*. Caroline had been the dead-last thing on his mind, and something told him it wouldn't exactly have fostered the trust they were build-ing if he hadn't gotten that tidbit on the table. And even now, he realized there were details he should fill in. Specifics that didn't actually change anything, but—hell, Megan's capitula-tion in giving this marriage a try had been a close thing. Too close. He wasn't willing to risk some unfortunate chronology putting her off, at least not until they were on more solid ground.

"Can't believe you didn't introduce us yesterday. I want to

meet this woman…now that I know she didn't drag you down the aisle at knifepoint," Jeff clarified.

Connor grinned and started walking again, raising a hand when Megan turned his way, her too-wide smile doing too many things to him at once.

"Soon. For now, I'm ready to get her home."

"Good to hear it. But I want details. Start at the beginning."

"You'd been gone about thirty seconds when the 'gymnast' shows up at the table, with this whopper of a line."

"The gymnast? *Dude!*"

Megan met him halfway and, apparently having overheard the last bit, arched an amused brow. Leaning toward the phone, she piped in, "I'm not a gymnast."

Connor ducked and dropped a quick kiss at her temple, relishing the faint blush in her cheeks. "Only, she's not a gymnast, and it's not actually a line…"

Megan woke to the steady *thud, thud* of Connor's heart beneath her ear, the constant weight of his arm around her waist and the whirl of a mind anxious to put sleep behind it.

After two nonstop days in Denver, they'd packed the bulk of her apartment, leaving only the barest essentials behind. Laughter and fun like she'd never known had punctuated intense negotiations, strict limits and hard deadlines as a plan for the next three months came together. Sleeping arrangements, travel and social obligations, their respective professional commitments and myriad other details of this life they were embarking on had to be addressed. With so much to do, and so many decisions to make…it had been after midnight when Connor finally carried her over the threshold of his spacious San Diego home and about five minutes after that when they'd collapsed into bed.

Now Megan was blinking the sleep from her eyes, a silly grin curving her lips as the phrase "Today is the first day of the rest of your life" came to mind. Squinting around the unfamiliar room, she located a clock at the far corner and winced at the realization *today* was beginning at the ungodly hour of four.

Megan made a stealthy escape from the bed and padded

down the stairs, flipping on one light after another as she tried to familiarize herself with a house not yet her home, searching for clues about the man she'd married along the way. What she'd discovered was an immaculately decorated showplace, where each room had a central piece of artwork around which everything else flowed. Horses in charcoal tore across an open plain in the massive study, a bronze figurine capturing the essence of a weary rider atop his mount was the central focus in a reading room, and aged leather behind glass in the living room revealed her husband had the heart of a cowboy.

Such a contrast to the clean lines and neat cut of his made-to-measure everything else. At least everything she'd seen so far. But perhaps that had just been Vegas.

There was so much left to learn.

Her mother's parting words from their previous morning's conversation whispered to her.

"You're going to have to step up your game if you want to hang on to this one..."

She shook her head. Some advice.

There was no game. There never had been.

She knew better, thanks to the lessons learned at her mother's knee.

Turning from the relic of the Old West, her gaze caught on the floor-to-ceiling glass doors making up the southwest wall. The inky black of the early hours had faded to blue and the landscape around them had begun to take shape. Palms stretched like dark cutouts against the morning sky and elusive streaks of white rushed the shores.

Slowly she stepped forward, wanting to put her mother's words and the memories they spurred behind her. Lose herself in the beauty revealed by the approach of the rising sun. Only, the past had already taken hold. All the "daddies" who'd walked through her life. The great guys Gloria Scott had been willing to do anything—*be anyone*—to keep ahold of. The wild changes to her mother's personality and personal goals heralding the arrival of each new man. Megan's own determination not to let this one get too close—no matter how nice or fun he was—because it wouldn't last. It never lasted. The tug at her little girl's nerves once things started to slip. The sidelong looks, the downward pull of a mouth. The hope that maybe she was wrong. That maybe if she was good enough, if she tried hard enough, this one wouldn't leave.

But they all did.

Eugene, Charlie, Pete, Rubin, Zeke, Jose and Dwayne. Seven husbands come and gone, and still her mom hadn't figured it out. A person couldn't *make* something last if it wasn't meant to, like a person couldn't *be* someone they weren't. And trying only prolonged the inevitable.

Some were easier to let go. And some—she let out a heavy sigh as the memory of sun-crinkled eyes winking at her from across a worn dock squeezed her heart—the echoes of their absence were so deeply ingrained in her psyche they touched every relationship she'd ever attempted.

Her fingers trailed the wood frame of the sliders as a thread of anxious tension stitched through Megan's belly. In spite of her determination not to, was she just repeating her mother's mistakes?

She'd married a man she'd known for less than a day. A man who'd been so sold on the woman he met that first night—a night she couldn't remember—he was determined not to let her get away. Sure, Connor thought he knew her. But what if he was wrong? What if she hadn't been herself and he was so caught up in the hard-won victory he was after that he simply hadn't realized it yet?

How long before he saw past the illusion of who he wanted her to be—and actually saw *her*?

Would it be within the span of this trial or would it be after she'd finally let herself believe—

"You're up early."

Megan spun around to find Connor watching her from the hall, a pair of light cotton gray pajama bottoms hanging dangerously low on his trim hips. The bare expanse of his cut chest was emphasized by the casual way he'd leaned one arm at the edge of the open frame doorway.

"So are you."

God, he was gorgeous with his mess of silky hair standing every which way and a day's growth roughing up the perfection of his square-cut jaw, giving him a sort of roguish look to match the smile and eyes.

"My bed got lonely," he offered with a wink that did something crazy to her insides and reminded her of how impossible it was not to get caught up in this man's convictions when they were together.

He believed in them. Was so ready to take that headlong dive into their future. Made it seem so simple.

Just jump.

When he looked at her the way he was right then, it made her want to jump too. Made her want everything he was offering. But wanting something didn't necessarily mean it was right. She had to keep her head.

"Lonely."

He grinned. "Yeah, well, I also figured you might like a tour of your new home. Some coffee maybe?"

She let out an involuntary moan. "Coffee, yes, please."

Laughing, he walked over and caught her hand. "My ego's demanding the next time you make that noise, it's not going to be because of coffee. Come on."

In the kitchen, she rifled through the freezer as Connor got the pot brewing.

"I'm not much of a cook, in case I didn't mention it already, but frozen waffles I can do," she offered over her shoulder.

Connor closed in behind her, one arm reaching past to swing the freezer door shut. "In a minute."

Her heart skipped a beat and her belly fluttered.

"Connor," she warned, taking a step in retreat.

"Relax, sweetheart," he soothed, catching her hips and backing her to the neat square kitchen table, then popping her up to sit atop. "All I'm after is my previously agreed-upon good-morning kiss."

Their compromise on physical intimacy.

It had been a point of contention between them, with Megan

determined not to let seduction sway her thinking about the marriage, and Connor wanting—well, everything. In the end, neither of them had been interested in the kind of precedent three months of strictly platonic set—trial or not. So they'd settled on a daily kiss count of four, with good-morning, have-a-good-day, welcome-home and good-night kisses to be granted at the corresponding times.

Four. She could totally handle four kisses.

Her body warmed at the knowledge it was time to pay the piper.

Parting her knees, he stepped between them. Leaned in close. Closer. And closer still until he'd braced one hand on the hardwood behind her and wrapped the other around her waist, leaving Megan no choice but to cling to his shoulders.

"One kiss, Connor," she whispered, already feeling drugged by the sleepy bedroom scent of him.

"One kiss. Any way I want to take it."

Breathless, she stared up into his eyes. "And you want it on the breakfast table."

Letting out a low groan, Connor ran the bridge of his nose along the line of her jaw to below her ear. "God, yes. But I'll settle for the kiss if it's all you're ready to give me."

"Just the kiss." She'd tried to keep the pleading quality from her tone, but she wanted to be reminded of the chemistry. The magic. What this was leading to if everything worked out. Or maybe all she wanted was Connor's mouth on hers again.

That cocky smile cranked another notch, Connor's lids dropping slumberously low. "We'll see."

And then she had it. The first soft rub of his lips against hers. The gentle, coaxing hint of the hot demand to come.

God, she wanted this to last.

CHAPTER TWELVE

"No sex?" Jeff coughed through the line.

Hands tightening on the wheel, knuckles going white, Connor hadn't missed the undertones of amusement, no matter how his friend tried to cover it.

Glad someone thought it was funny.

"Yeah, I can't believe it either. But Megan…" He took a slow breath, glancing out over the cliffs down to the ocean beyond before returning his attention to the road in front of him. He'd been so sure he had her with the daily make-out quota, because when they kissed—he slid a finger into his collar, freed the button and loosened his tie—they *really* kissed. But true to her word, Megan held strong. "She doesn't want her judgment clouded while she figures things out."

"Right. I get it. Blow-your-mind bedroom antics have a tendency to confuse priorities. Give meaning to the meaningless. Make things seem 'special' when really they aren't. Smart."

Connor ground down his molars, not exactly sure what response he'd wanted from Jeff…but certain it wasn't this.

"So aside from the fact that your fresh-from-the-chapel wife finds you totally resistible, how's the *rest* of married life treating you?"

"Good. No surprises." Not really, anyway. "Megan's more reserved than she came across our first night. And she's somewhat preoccupied with making sure I know what I'm getting into. You know, listing faults in the name of full disclosure because she doesn't want to risk me stumbling over some deal breaker once she's committed."

After a few seconds' pause, the joking tone was gone. "Deal breakers?"

"Relax," Connor assured. "Minor stuff. Quirks mostly."

After all, he couldn't care less if she wasn't a stellar cook or had a tendency to go overboard when she picked up a new hobby. But he sure as hell cared whether the woman he married was going to be straight with him. And every time they were together, she showed him she was.

Even so, he wanted her confidence back. The faith she'd put in herself and him when she'd spoken her vows. But every time she revealed some other fault, waiting a beat to see how he'd handle the news, whether it would shake him, he was reminded how that faith had been wrung out of her like a bar rag.

Didn't matter. She'd see soon enough. And until then...well, he really couldn't complain. She was strong. Smart. She knew how to protect herself.

"She makes me laugh. And she's exceptionally easy to be with. Easy to talk to." Easy to look at and easy to think about. Maybe even a little too easy on that last count.

But it was to be expected.

Megan was a challenge. And though he'd gotten her to give their marriage a chance, he knew she wasn't sold. Which meant she was an unfinished project. A deal hovering on the brink of closure. Damn it, she was an itch yet to be scratched. He wanted her, and until he knew she was securely his, she'd be occupying more of his mind than he would typically allot to a relationship.

"Man, I'm glad you found a woman you can talk to. I know you'd always figured on a marriage that was more of a merger. And after Caro—"

"Look, I'm about home." Connor slowed at the driveway, waiting for the security gate and garage to open. "Time to wear down the wife."

"Got it." Jeff laughed, not taking the abrupt end to the conversation personally. If he had something to say, he'd make sure he got another chance to say it. "And good luck… Sounds like you're going to need it."

Connor cut the call and jumped out of the car, a slow grin spreading to his lips as his mind latched on to the last sight he'd had of his wife before he left for work. He knew she wouldn't look like the sexy kitten she'd been that morning, purring under the kiss he'd pressed against her lips before she'd been quite awake. Sleep mussed and warm. The silky pajamas she'd been wearing shaping over her nipples and riding high toward her ribs.

Small wonder she'd been on his mind the past eleven hours.

She'd be dressed by now. Probably all neat and tidy. Still, he couldn't quite kick the salacious happenings taking place in the not-so-far-back of his mind. Silky, sleep-mussed happenings wrapped up in a welcome-home, I've-been-aching-for-you-all-day kind of kiss.

Yeah, fat chance.

Closing the door behind him, he called down the hall with a facetious "Honey, I'm home."

The silence echoed back to him as he dropped his keys on the glass-topped table and kept walking toward the stairs. The second floor was dark and empty, with only a single dim bulb illuminated at the top of the flight. The third floor too. His brow furrowed as he checked his phone for messages. None.

It wasn't as if returning to an empty house was a new experience for him, but with Megan living there, he'd expected… something different.

Not that he was disappointed. He'd wanted an independent woman who wouldn't make him feel guilty about the schedule he kept or as if her life was tied to his.

Wish granted!

Only walking through the empty house that had never felt lonely to him before, he had to concede a week into their marriage that he hadn't anticipated getting his wish would suck quite this way.

Midway down the darkened hall, Connor paused, just outside Megan's office door. A sliver of light leaked through the seam, and from within came the quiet yet distinct sound of keys tapping.

She was here.

Turning the knob, Connor opened the door to Megan's sanctuary…and discovered his silk-clad morning fantasy staring hard at the monitor as her fingers assaulted the keyboard in front of her.

The sexiness of her sleep-rumpled look had gone mildly stale throughout the day, and yet Connor couldn't take his eyes off her. She was intense, focused. And bobbing her lovely head ever so slightly to the beat of whatever she had pumping into her ears through those hot-pink little earbuds.

Never in a million years would he have expected to come home to a scene like this if he'd married Caro. She'd have been polished and primped. Attentive in the distant way he'd become so familiar with. Making small talk, much as they did with strangers through a cocktail party.

And he'd never have really known—in all honesty, would never have really cared—where her head was at.

Not like this, he thought with a bemused smile. Right now, he knew exactly where Megan's head was. Deep in her work. The project she'd been waiting on must finally have come in.

Standing unnoticed in the doorway, he considered his alternatives.

He could walk across the room and take advantage of her distraction. Pull her blond mess to the side and start with her neck, close his mouth over the spectacularly sensitive spot behind her ear and work his way forward from there…

Or he could go order some dinner—because based on what he was seeing, he'd bet food hadn't even crossed her mind. And when he took his kiss…he wanted Megan paying attention.

Running a hand over the back of his neck, he turned away.

"Connor?"

Her voice was overloud and she was staring at him, looking adorably confused.

He tapped his ear and she pulled the bud from her own.

"Hey, gorgeous. How was your day?"

He'd meant the compliment, but Megan seemed to have taken it tongue in cheek—her face blanching as her hands went to her hair and then those silky pajamas that told more secrets than they kept.

Only, then the most interesting thing happened. That flash of embarrassment faded and something that looked a lot like challenge took its place. "I get caught up in my work...I lose track. It can be irritating for some people."

Ah, more with the disclosures. Whatever it took.

"You near a good stopping point if I call in Chinese?" he asked, sensing the time to wrap things up would put her in a better place to break for the night. It was how it would be with him.

"You wouldn't mind?" Her eyes shot back to his, infinitely softer than they'd been only seconds before.

"I better not—tables'll be turned soon enough." No question. "I'll order and grab a quick shower. Meet me downstairs when you're ready."

At her slight frown, Connor stopped. "Something wrong?"

"You don't want your kiss?"

"Oh, I want it," he assured, giving in to the grin hovering around his lips. "But not until I've got your undivided attention. So wrap it up."

The door closed and Megan stared at her computer, relieved by Connor's easy acceptance of her distraction and yet unable to shake the doubts. The sense that if it wasn't this that opened Connor's eyes to a future he didn't want, then it would be something else. Eventually.

She didn't want to think that way. There was so much *right* between them, and yet, a part of her couldn't buy in. A part of her saw the calm mask Connor wore when she showed him something he, by all rights, ought to dislike—and wondered what lay hidden beneath.

Sure, getting tied up with work this evening wasn't such a big deal. But it didn't seem to matter what she said or did. As if no bad habit or personal shortcoming even registered. As if maybe Connor was so determined to prove how perfectly suited for this marriage they were that he'd turn a blind eye to anything that didn't fit.... Until one day he wouldn't be able to do it anymore.

What happened then?

God, she wanted to believe. But with so much at stake, she needed Connor to acknowledge more than some illusion of perfection. She needed to know he was really seeing her.

CHAPTER THIRTEEN

"SHE MADE YOU WHAT?" Jeff choked through the line.

Connor shook his head at Megan's latest attempt to confront him with a reality she expected him to reject. *Her latest failed attempt.*

"Creamed tuna on mashed potatoes. With peas." Canned, boxed and frozen. He knew because she'd left the containers in plain view on the counter. "Apparently it's one of those old family favorites she just has to have once in a while."

"No. Way."

The last time he'd heard that kind of awe in Jeff's voice, the man had just watched a supermodel bungee off the Verzasca Dam in Ticino, Switzerland, tossing him a wink and blown kiss before taking air.

"Damn, she's serious about shaking you."

Connor bristled, reining in the growl currently threatening his cool. "If she's so serious she ought to come up with something more substantial than dinner. Like I'm going to bolt because she served me less than five-star cuisine. *Come on.*"

It was an insult to both of them.

"You ate it?"

"Of course I ate it," he scoffed, surprised Jeff would even ask. "She made it for me."

And he'd finished every bite, as if it was manna from heaven.

Then giving in to a reluctant chuckle, he added, "But I have to admit that gelatinous puddle—*which even Megan didn't eat,* by the way—was without question the worst thing I've ever shoveled into my mouth."

"Dude."

Half an hour later, thoughts of tests and frustrations had been put aside. Connor strode into the kitchen, working his tie and collar open, stare locked on the delectable curve of Megan's backside, showcased in a pair of clingy yoga pants as she—oh, hell—checked what looked like a lasagna in the oven...but smelled, wow, more than a shade off.

Not. Again.

"Hey, gorgeous," he said, announcing his presence a second before sliding his hands over the sweet curve of her hips. He needed a reminder as to why he was going to choke down the coming atrocity. An incentive of sorts.

With his hands coasting over her hips and waist, she swung the steel door closed and started to turn as he said, "How about my welcome-home— Gah!"

Connor's head jerked back as he was hit with the one-two punch of Megan's smiling face covered in some kind of bottom-of-the-vegetable-drawer-looking half-dry paste...and the accompanying rotting stink of it.

"Your kiss?" She laughed, patting him gently on the chest and then casting him a mischievous wink as she stepped out of his hold. "Sorry to surprise you with the swamp-thing mask, but I do one weekly," she offered with a little shrug.

"Weekly." God, he couldn't even imagine coming face-to-face with this odor on a regular basis. Daring a closer look, he leaned in and ran his finger along one tacky cheek. "What's it do?"

Megan shrugged. "Um...well, it tightens your pores. And removes impurities. Keeps the skin looking smoother. Younger. More healthy."

Hmm. Half the time he was with her she wasn't wearing any makeup, and she was *beautiful*. Her skin flawless with those pale freckles sprinkled around it. Maybe it was the mask?

"Interesting." Then waving his hand in front of his face, he asked, "So what other beauty secrets should I be looking forward to?"

He'd never asked any of the other women he'd dated about their mysterious feminine rituals, but then, he'd never been curious before. And of course, he'd never been this up close and personal to one either.

Arms crossed, she gave him a scrutinizing look. After a beat, "Waxing."

"Really." His gaze drifted down the line of her body, curiosity on the rise about every potentially smooth, bare strip of skin.

This time it was Megan circling a hand round her face, her all-challenge smile gone full tilt. "Really."

Confusion first. Then understanding. His chin snapped back. "Really?"

Megan arched a delicate brow at him. "Why, it doesn't bother you, does it?"

He might have mistaken her look as playful—if not for the glint of steel in her eyes.

His good humor and amused intrigue shut down.

Another test.

Three weeks and he hadn't proven a damn thing to her. Hadn't made the slightest headway in easing her concerns. And it was starting to chafe. Pull and rub against the seams of who he was—to the point where something had to give.

But not him.

"I know what you're doing, Megan."

She stared at him a beat. Bracing.

Good idea. She was going to need it, because he had a point to make.

He started toward her, letting his mind peel away the layers of defense she'd erected. The mask, the tests, until the only thing he saw was the woman who'd stared up at him that first night. "I know what I want, Megan."

She was backed against the counter, the breath rushing past her lips in a way that called to his most primitive self.

"And if you think the threat of some smelly mask or not-quite-so-sexy waxing ritual is going to keep me from getting it…" He stroked the shell of her ear, tucked a few wayward strands behind as he took the caress down the line of her neck.

He leaned farther into her space and let the edge back into his voice. "…you've got another think coming."

Wide eyes within a flaking mask of putrid green held with his.

Ready not only to meet her challenge, but raise hers as well—Connor closed in, breathing solely through his mouth. "I'll have my kiss now."

Okay, that hadn't gone the way she'd intended it. Not by a long shot.

Breathless and trembling with unfulfilled desire, T-shirt bunched around one elbow, Megan stared down at herself draped across the polished granite of the center island in utter disbelief as Connor coolly strode out of the kitchen. *Whistling to himself!*

As though he'd claimed some victory instead of crawling off this countertop himself, covered in disgusting flecks of algae mask, his tailor-made shirt missing half its buttons and the tent in his suit pants threatening irreparable damage to his fly.

She'd resisted him!

Granted, it had taken her a while to come to her senses. And possibly only then because in the midst of that tempest of passion, she'd opened her eyes to catch her green-faced reflection in the gleaming metal of a countertop bowl. But still, after a few breathless attempts, she'd managed his name. And a few minutes later, she'd even unhooked her ankles from the small of his back and said no.

Like she meant it. Sort of.

Connor had delivered one last, soul-searing kiss and then… dismounted.

Whistling.

Pfft.

So this revolting mask—that even she could barely stand but used religiously because, despite the stink, nothing worked like it—wasn't enough to throw Connor off his game. In truth, she hadn't really expected it to be.

The man she'd married was no lightweight. He was goal driven. Unafraid of confrontation, hard work or the pungent scent of swamp.

Megan swallowed hard.

She wanted him. But every time she found herself confronted with his unflappable, easy confidence—his smooth sell and I-don't-back-down stare—she couldn't stop the thoughts slithering through her mind.

He held too much sway, made all the right promises and left her feeling more vulnerable than she ever had before. Connor wouldn't acknowledge anything out of line with his goal. He wouldn't respond in any believable way. Which terrified her. Because by refusing to acknowledge who *she really was*, and curbing his every response, he was actually preventing her from seeing *the real him*, as well.

But she couldn't make herself walk away. Because for every too-easily-dismissed fault, there were a hundred instances of sincerity. Moments too pure, too intense, to be anything but genuine.

God, she had to be careful.

Megan couldn't believe it had come to this.

She knew which waffles Connor liked. Not only did she know which waffles he liked—she *cared* about which waffles he liked. And even worse—she'd spent the past ten minutes standing in the open door of the frozen-breakfast section determined to find waffles even better. So she could be the one to offer the best damn toaster waffle her husband had ever wrapped his tongue around.

Oh, this was bad. Very bad.

And totally embarrassing, now that she stopped to think about it. They were waffles, for crying out loud.

Feeling suddenly conspicuous, she glanced down the aisle half expecting to find a crowd of snickering onlookers taking bets on which brand she'd opt for, only, instead her focus caught on a head of short salt-and-pepper curls topping a face she hadn't seen in the two decades that had weathered it.

Her breath leaked out of her in a thin, chilled wisp. "Pete."

She blinked, stepping forward before she'd even thought to curb the impulse. It couldn't be him. In all the years, it was never actually him. But this time…she could swear it was.

Heart pounding, she felt a bubble of laughter rising in her chest. Did she hug him? Shake his hand? Tell him that even now she could feel the way she'd missed him all those years ago.

He had to live around here. Though, the way he loved to travel, maybe he was just passing through. Either way, she was already reaching for him when he said, "Say, Sprout, whadiya think about chocolate with peanut butter and marshmallows?"

She stopped, too confused to make sense of the words she was hearing.

Only, then he glanced over at her and let out a bark of surprised laughter as he took a quick step back.

"Oh, heck, pardon me, young lady. For a minute I thought you were my daughter." His eyes crinkled around the edges. "Serves me right, not looking at who I'm talking to."

Just then, a heavily pregnant woman rounded the corner rubbing her belly with one hand as she scanned her grocery list. "No marshmallows, Dad, but I'm down with the peanut butter."

Pete gave her a nod and reached into the case to grab another carton. He dropped it into his cart and then looked back at Megan expectantly.

Because she was staring. And he had no idea who she was.

Of course he didn't. Though he looked so much the same it hurt her heart to see him, she'd been a little girl the last time he saw her. "Pete, I'm Megan Scott. I mean I was Megan Scott. I got married. It's Megan Reed now."

Heat burned through her cheeks as she realized how much it pleased her to be able to tell him that she'd married. To think that she might be able to introduce him to Connor. They'd get along. She knew they would. It hadn't really struck her until just that second, but there were actually a number of similarities between them.

Only, then her racing thoughts ground to a halt and all that excited energy died as the furrow between Pete's eyes dug deep.

"Megan…*Scott*?" He glanced over his shoulder at his daughter, standing a few feet off wearing a pleasant smile on her face, and then snapped his fingers, looking back at Megan. "From the bank over on First?"

CHAPTER FOURTEEN

HE'D BEEN LOOKING for a fight, that much Connor could admit. Pulling around the corner to the house, he'd felt the gathering tension through his back and neck, the same kind of jacked pulse he got before walking into a major negotiation. The fact that his system was ramping for conflict in anticipation of seeing his wife only made it worse.

There hadn't been any new "tests," but the emotional distance, the guarded looks and speculation when she thought he wasn't looking—and hell, sometimes even when she knew he was—had only increased. Something was coming.

Only, then he'd pulled through the security gate and seen the open garage, Megan's car parked and her still in the driver's seat. A quiet alarm began to sound in the back of his mind as he cut the engine and jumped out. All that jacked-up ready-to-go morphed into protective instinct.

This wasn't right.

Rounding the car, he came up to her window and stopped short at the sight of tear-streaked cheeks and a bleak stare. And for the first time since they'd met, he saw something other than how strong Megan was. Beneath all that toughness was something fragile. Something she didn't show to the world but here and now she couldn't hide from him.

His gut knotted hard as the first question slammed through his head.

Had he done this to her? Pushed her too far? Asked too much? Broken her?

Heart pounding, he forced himself to knock on the glass instead of ripping the door off its hinges to get to her. Find out what happened, if he was to blame. Make sure Megan wasn't hurt. *Physically.*

She jumped in her seat as he opened the door, her eyes darting around the interior of the car before landing on him. The arms that had been hanging limply in her lap jerked up, and then she was wiping at her cheeks, mumbling some kind of unintelligible apology as she emerged from her daze.

Resting a staying hand on her shoulder, Connor crouched beside her seat, searching for clues in a face his wife was rapidly trying to clear. Only, with each sweep of her thumbs, another tear slipped free.

"Megan, what's going on, honey?"

She sucked in a shaky breath, swallowed and then bowed her head. "It's so stupid. I'm sorry. I shouldn't be like this. I just… saw someone I used to know."

Connor's muscles bunched. It wasn't him, then, making her cry—and the relief he felt over that was immense. But it was nothing compared to the outrage pouring through him that someone else had done this to his wife.

Someone she used to know.

"Barry?" The idiot who'd run off and married another woman when he'd been making plans with Megan. The one he'd believed wasn't important enough to merit this kind of sorrow. Did the guy have some kind of hold over her heart Connor hadn't realized?

Was he in California to get Megan back?

She shook her head, valiantly trying to force a smile to lips that couldn't bear the weight of it. "No. His name is Pete. And for about a year, a very long time ago, he was my dad."

Her dad.

Connor was at a loss. He knew Megan had been raised by her mother, a serial bride who didn't have much of a track record when it came to keeping husbands. Megan never talked about any of the guys her mother had married, and he'd gotten the sense they hadn't been of particular importance in her life. Only, now he was wondering just exactly how off base he'd been.

"What happened?"

"He didn't remember me." Megan winced and closed her eyes. When she opened them again, she was blinking fast. Giving her head one of those thought-jarring shakes. As though she was physically trying to throw off the emotion. She wanted to be strong. And hell, he admired her for it. But as the tears continued to fall, the heartbreak in her eyes was unmistakable. And damn it, he'd seen that kind of pain before. Knew the kind of soul-deep wound it stemmed from. Feared it.

The kind where a person's whole heart was tied up in the hope of something they understood they couldn't have. The kind another person couldn't fix or fill or make up for...could only pray they were strong enough to withstand.

She was strong.

"Sweetheart, I'm sorry."

"It was so long ago. I don't know how I expected he would remember me, but I was practically ready to throw my arms around—" Her voice broke, and she glanced away.

Damn. Megan looked so lost and vulnerable, he couldn't stand it. Needed to do something. Ground her in some way.

Taking her hand, he stroked a thumb over her knuckles. "Let's go inside."

She nodded and he stepped back, helping her from the car. Her eyes shifted toward the house, and he half expected her to simply draw herself up and walk away. Retreat to a place he couldn't reach her.

Only, then she closed her eyes and *turned into him*, pressing her face against the center of his chest, so there was nothing to do but wrap his arms around her trembling shoulders and hold her close. Stare down in disbelief as Megan clung to him.

Pulling her in closer, he laid his cheek against the silky strands at the top of her head and stroked a hand over her back.

"It's okay, sweetheart. I've got you," he promised, rocked by the depth of meaning behind his words. He wanted to protect her in a way he'd never experienced before. And that she wanted his protection and comfort—could accept it—was profoundly satisfying.

"I told him my name and he couldn't place it. I mentioned my mom and the connection clicked. But it was…so awkward."

Connor ushered Megan inside and up to their room where they lay in bed together with her head resting in the crook of his arm. They spoke in hushed tones, watching the shadows fill in around them as the light faded and the quiet of night replaced the cacophony of day.

"They were all good guys," Megan whispered in response to the question he'd just asked, her breath warming the spot above his heart still damp from her tears. "That was the thing. Mom never picked jerks we could only pray would take off sooner rather than later. They were all nice men we hoped would stay, even though deep down I knew they wouldn't."

"There were seven?"

"Seven she married."

Which meant there were more she hadn't.

He couldn't imagine what it would be like for a little girl to have a revolving door of father figures passing through her life that way, or how her mother could have let it go on. But he knew all about women who couldn't control their hearts—even for the sake of their children. Even for the sake of themselves. At least Megan's mother had been resilient enough to bounce back. Move on.

"When she brought Pete home, I barely even spoke to him. It was terrible, but I think it had only been a couple of months since the one before had left, and I didn't want to—care, I guess. Only, Pete was sort of relentless. He wanted to win me over—do everything to make this new family work. So he told jokes and stories. Took me fishing. Talked to me and actually listened to what I said. He made me feel…special. Like I was more than just the kid who came with the woman he'd married. Like I was his friend too. Thinking back on it now, though, I wonder if maybe it wasn't more a case of me being the perfect project for finding common ground with a wife with whom he otherwise didn't share much."

Connor tightened his hold around Megan's shoulders, giving her whatever time she needed to go on.

"When he left I thought it would be…different. I thought he might stop back so he could say goodbye to me. Maybe call to tell me he missed me or that he was sorry he had to go. But he didn't and I figured it was because of my mom's rule about severing ties. Still, he'd said he loved me, so I kept waiting and hoping. And maybe I never stopped, because when I saw him at the store this afternoon, I was so— Oh, God, Connor, I was such a fool."

"No, Megan. Not you." That she even thought so— Connor silently cursed this Pete and Megan's mother both for what they'd put her through. For not recognizing the impact their careless actions would have. The guy told Megan he loved her. He made her believe it and then walked away. A little girl whose tender heart had already been bruised time and again.

And the worst of it—the part that churned in Connor's gut—was the knowledge that in no small way, he owed Gloria Scott and this string of faithless men a debt of gratitude. If their repeated abuse hadn't broken her ability to trust in love enough to surrender to it, this woman never would have settled for this partnership he had to offer her. She'd have found someone years ago to love her the way she deserved and they'd be married with a half-dozen kids in tow.

He might not be able to give her a storybook romance with love everlasting, but he'd make damn sure she had everything else. He'd be constant. The man she could count on. They'd get past this trial, and time would show her. She'd see.

Megan woke on a gasp, her eyes flying wide as she jolted upright. She scanned the empty bed and room around her. Tried to get a hold on the reality that was now, even as the nightmare she'd been fleeing pressed at her mind.

She'd been running, lost in the kind of fog only the dreamworld could conjure. Searching for Connor, knowing it was a mistake, but unable to stop herself.

And then he was there. His arms warm around her, his hushed nonsense a confusing comfort at her ear.

She looked up to ask him what he meant, and it was Pete's face speaking with Connor's voice. "Don't worry, I'm going to win you over."

Desperately she looked around and, again finding Connor across the void, called out to him.

He smiled, the lines at the corners of his eyes etching deeper as she watched. "I don't remember you."

Throwing back the covers, she pushed the nightmare away. Told herself it was just her head processing the mess yesterday had been. Except instead of settling down, the panic she'd experienced in her sleep was on the rise.

She needed to find Connor. Needed to—

"Hey, you're awake."

She spun toward the door where he'd come to stop with that same casual arm slung up around the top of the frame. Jeans and a soft T-shirt tempted her with hints of the powerful body hidden beneath. But it was the ever-elusive half smile that held her, making her feel the coming loss deep in the center of her chest.

She swallowed, watching as Connor's easy posture went straight and the smile slid away with all the warmth that had been in his eyes.

His voice was hard when he spoke. "No."

"Connor, I'm sorry." Wringing her hands, she took a tentative step in his direction. "I can't do this."

"Bull," he fired back, the spark of temper igniting his outrage so completely it was as though the tinder had been set, waiting in place. "You haven't even tried!"

"That's not true. I have. I've been trying for a month. But it's no use. I'm not settling into a life I feel like I can keep. I don't—" She broke off, shifting her gaze from the accusation in his.

God, she didn't want him looking at her that way...she didn't want to deserve it.

"You don't *what*, Megan? If this is it, then let's just own it all. Say it."

Fists balling at her sides, she fought back the pain rising in her chest and did as he asked. "I don't trust you."

"Of course not. I've been honest, up-front and straightforward with you from the word go." Connor pushed off the wall, raking a savage hand through his hair. "Yeah, I wouldn't trust me either."

Megan watched in despair as he stormed from one end of the room to the other and back, his outrage blasting her like gale-force winds.

"It's not you," she swore. "It's me."

Shooting her a condemning look, he let out a harsh laugh. "Is that so? Not a single thing I could do, huh?"

"No." He'd already done too much. Been too perfect. Too perfect to believe he was real.

Connor crossed his arms and stared down at her. "You never wanted to be convinced. From the start you've been looking for any excuse you can find to justify walking away before you had to risk...anything."

Her mouth dropped open. It wasn't true. She just—she—

She was suddenly angry. Really angry.

At herself. At Connor. At Pete and her mother and every event that had brought her to this horrible moment.

"How am I supposed to risk everything on someone who isn't real!"

"What the hell are you talking about?"

"You don't react to anything, Connor! You don't get mad. You don't get frustrated. No matter what I throw at you, no matter what I say, it's like all you're focused on is the goal at the finish line. Secure the wife and nothing else matters. I never see anything but your unflappable calm and easy charm. You're always so *reasonable*. Always with the *rational* approach. The *perfect* solution to any problem. And it's impossible to believe, because *no one* is that perfect, Connor. That's why I can't trust you. That's why I have to leave!"

CHAPTER FIFTEEN

CONNOR STARED DOWN at his wife, absorbing this final revelation.

He'd been vowing to give her everything he had, but... *nothing would be enough.*

He'd thought there couldn't be anything worse than the helpless sense of failure and inadequacy that marked the first thirteen years of his life. When no good grade, lost tooth or scored goal was enough to push the heartbreak from his mother's eyes—not when every milestone achieved was simply a reminder of the man who was missing them all. When Connor's dependence—his very existence—hadn't weighed heavily enough to compete with the bottle of sleeping pills she'd taken to end the pain. But now, to realize he'd simply exchanged one woman with a hurt he couldn't touch for another with a doubt he couldn't overcome... *Damn it,* what was he doing? What kind of messed-up psychosis kept him coming back to this impossible place—when he'd spent his entire adult life actively working to avoid it?

He should let her go.

Except then he thought about the desolate look in Megan's eyes the night before. That instant when he'd been sure she would turn away...but instead she'd clung to him and cried against his chest. Took his comfort. His strength.

And woke up the next morning ready to run.

To hell with this.

"You want to see a reaction, Megan? You want something real?" He stalked slowly toward her, letting the anger pulse off him in waves. "I'm furious. Only, I sure as hell didn't get this way because my wife took the time to cook me a dinner. In fact, it's not any of that trivial nonsense you've been shoving at me. Because—truth?—on the scale of significance, that stuff doesn't even register. What has me pushed past the boiling point...what has me really, really *upset* is learning the woman I thought was so incredibly strong I married her on the spot...is actually a *quitter* who runs from challenge, a *coward* too afraid to even try, a *liar* who makes promises she won't keep and a *cynic* too bitter to believe what's right in front of her face. Is that real enough for you?"

Megan's lips parted on a gasp, her eyes blinking time and again, as though she couldn't quite believe what she'd just seen. What he'd said. Then, barely a whisper, "You're wrong."

Connor shook his head, wishing he were.

"I don't think so. But I'll tell you what I am...mad as hell. *At you.* Right now. More angry than I've ever been at a woman I was in a relationship with. But—and this is the important part, baby, so listen up—*I'm not the one ready to leave.* I'm the one trying to get you mad enough to fight back. To throw down your gloves, get up in my face and prove me wrong. I want you to stay because what we could have is worth fighting for. And if that's not *real* enough, damn it, I want you to stay for this too—" Grabbing her shoulders, he pulled her into a hard, searing kiss.

It was too brief. Didn't satisfy more than the most base claim. And when he pulled back, ire still surging hot through his veins, he met Megan's eyes, daring her next response.

She stared up at him through air thick with tension, her expression stunned, hands resting at his chest and abdomen.

"You're *really* angry."

"Incensed," he assured, not just trying to sweet-talk her, but meaning it completely.

"And you still want me." Her fingers closed around the fabric of his T-shirt. "Us." Her pupils shot wide and the breath trembling past her lips whispered of unfulfilled desire. "This."

Heat licked across the space between them, burning away his restraint until there was nothing left but the single soul-deep truth that had been at the heart of it from the start. "Beyond reason or rationale."

And then there was only the hard press of one body against the next. Megan's mouth opened beneath the crush of his own. Her hands grappling to get higher, to wind tight in his hair, as he flattened her against the wall, hoisting her legs around his hips.

This was the kiss from that first night. This was the reality-shattering, blood-burning, hungry demand for more that had him ready to walk over coals to get it.

This was the woman he married.

Then, without breaking the contact of their lips, Megan told him what he'd been aching to hear. "I'm not a coward and I'm not a liar."

The sweet taste of her claim rushed over his tongue, and he returned it with his own guttural demand. "Prove it."

Another kiss and this time her tongue rubbed against his, soft and wet and so damn eager it stoked their desire to fever pitch.

Megan's restless hands stole down his back, grasping at the cotton of his shirt and tugging it high as Connor braced her against the wall, reaching overhead fast to the bunched fabric and jerking it off. Swooping in to the kiss he couldn't get enough of, Connor stopped at the barrier of Megan's delicate fingers between their lips.

Pulling them free so only that scant half inch remained, she spoke again. "I'm not a quitter."

He caught the back of her head with his palm and held her still to search those beautiful blue eyes. "Then stay, Megan. Stay and give us the chance we deserve."

Megan's arms linked tight around his neck.

"I'm sorry," she whispered urgently against his ear. "You were right about what I've been doing. Focusing on what could go wrong instead of appreciating what's right. I thought if I showed you the worst of who I was—" She broke off, shaking her head before looking back at him imploringly. "I've been trying to play it so smart, but all I've been is stupid and scared."

His hands moved to her waist, holding her tight as though

she weren't already holding him. As though he couldn't quite believe…she was actually fighting for them.

"Megan, tell me what you want." He could give it to her. Whatever she needed. Anything.

Her eyes, so wide and honest and deep, searched his and then darkened as they dropped to his mouth, lingered there for one agonizing beat. "I want *you.*"

Megan's head fell to the side as Connor devoured her neck, his mouth moving over her with a carnal intensity he'd shielded her from through every previous encounter they'd shared. All this time she'd been so sure he was giving her seduction his best effort, when in truth he'd been the one holding back.

This…she never would have been able to resist.

Standing in her panties at the edge of the bed, Connor wearing only those sexy boxers that made her mouth water, she trembled at the feel of her palms sliding over the terrain of his bare chest. The hard ridges of his abdomen ticking tight beneath her fingertips.

His body was so perfect she didn't know where to touch first, what to taste.

All of him.

That was what she wanted.

What she needed.

"I'm going to make love to you, Megan." His palms coasted over the lines of her body, leaving a path of warm friction sensitized in their wake. "With my hands…"

God, his touch was so good.

"…with my mouth…" His lips closed over the sensitive hollow at her collarbone, the gentle suction making her groan and squirm.

"Please."

"…with my body…"

And then he was guiding her to the bed, his broad chest meeting hers in one teasing kiss of flesh before he held himself above her. His mouth blazed a trail of heat and need from her neck down to her breast.

"So beautiful, Megan," he murmured, his lips brushing back and forth over the straining bud of her nipple before circling it with the firm point of his tongue and then licking, slowly, lower.

Over her ribs.

Around the small well of her navel.

Across the slight jut of her hip bone.

And then along the scalloped edge of her panties.

All the while she watched, held rapt by the vision of this gorgeous man indulging in his free rein over her body.

His hands coasted over her hips, knees, calves, touching her reverently as though in truth he meant to cover every inch of skin. Fingers sliding around her ankles and then back up, it wasn't until he'd reached her knees she realized the strategic shift of his arms from the outside of her legs to the inside, and even as she watched, he was coaxing her knees farther apart, opening her to him as he dropped kisses down the lacy V at the center of her panties, teasing her through the fabric with the warm wash of his breath…the press of his kiss.

"Oh, God, Connor," she moaned at the firm stroke of his tongue over the silky panel covering her.

Running his lips back and forth across the damp of her panties, he groaned. "I love it when you say my name right."

She gave in to a breathless laugh at his words, but then lost hold of the thought at the next wet stroke of his tongue.

A needy ache was building low in her belly, a tension without limit.

Fingers moving into the strands of his hair, she tried to urge him upward. "I want—"

Catching her wrists, he guided them back to their previous position above her. Holding her there for a beat that said *stay* more clearly than the voiced word itself.

Connor's fingers curled around her panties to peel them from her hips and slip them off her legs. His eyes, dark with hunger and glinting with determination, were mesmerizing as they met hers.

"I'm going to kiss you like this, sweetheart…the way I've wanted to from the start. Long and slow and deep…" he said, the sensual threat of his wicked half smile doing things even his touch hadn't accomplished.

Then, with a look so devilish she shivered, he added, "And French."

"Connor!" she gasped at the first wet velvet rub of his tongue. But the only reply was another hot lick. Her hands flew to his hair, his shoulders, the bed beside her hips, grasping and desperate beneath the most exquisite openmouthed kiss she'd ever experienced.

It was thorough. Spectacular. Her body was on fire around the slow thrusts, the curling licks and languorous strokes of his tongue. Then he was touching her at the same time. Circling his thumb at her opening and then slowly, firmly pressing inside as his kiss concentrated on the throbbing center of her need.

"Oh, God!" she cried out at the feel of him both inside her body and out.

It had been so long since she'd had a man's attention this way, but never had it been like this.

Need coiled low in her belly, each deliberate thrust of Connor's thumb intensifying the sensation until her hips were rising to meet him. Her pleasure cresting.

Her breath broke into ragged pants.

She was almost there. Sinking her teeth into the swell of her bottom lip to keep from screaming, Megan gripped the bedspread beneath her.

"Let go, Megan. I want to hear you." Another deliberate lick through the center of her, this one spiraling around that point of need so primed she didn't know if she could bear the exquisite pleasure the contact brought her.

Cries of need and desperation ripped past her lips, echoed around the walls of the room and rained down over them. Letting go with Connor like this was too good, too intense. So much more than she'd known was possible.

The pressure building within her touched every cell in her body, rubbed against the confines of her form and pushed steadily at the places she never expected it to reach. Places she thought far deeper, more tender and too forbidden for any man to find. Places she hadn't even known existed herself.

Her head thrashed, the sounds escaping her little more than incoherent pleas.

And then Connor closed his lips around that singular spot and gently sucked.

Starbursts exploded behind her eyes and she shattered. Her mind went blank and her body spasmed hard around and beneath Connor's touch as her thighs gripped his shoulders through wave after wave of release.

It was endless. Satisfaction like she'd never known. Loving like she'd never had. And yet it wasn't enough. Her body, so sated with pleasure, continued to ache. Everything inside her pulling toward the man who defied all logic.

Reaching out, she cupped Connor's hard jaw as he leaned over her, sliding his hand under her bottom to lift and reposition her at the center of the bed.

A moment later he'd rolled on a condom. Then, poised at her opening, he shifted his hips, penetrating her with the thick head of his erection. Gasping at the first shallow thrust stretching her wide, she clutched at his powerful shoulders.

He felt so good.

Connor rocked back, then eased forward again, setting a rhythm that took him incrementally deeper with each stroke until finally he was buried to the hilt within her, joining them as completely as two bodies could be.

Looking down into her eyes, he vowed, "No more holding back, Megan. Neither of us. I want it all."

So full she could barely breathe, she gasped the single word echoing through her heart, "Anything."

His mouth descended on hers, searing her with a hot kiss before breaking away. "Everything, Megan."

Megan opened her eyes to the sight of one large masculine hand engulfing her smaller one, both tucked close to her face. Hard muscle and powerful strength warmed her back and tangled with her limbs as steady breaths caressed the bare skin of her shoulder.

It was heaven.

And she'd almost thrown it away.

The heavy arm thrown over her side tightened, alerting her that Connor was awake. Turning to face him, she was struck by the intimacy of their heads sharing a single pillow as the late-morning sun spilled across the bed.

Looking into the too-symmetrical perfection of her husband's face, she asked, "Are you still mad at me?"

Connor rolled onto his back, but kept his face turned to hers so she saw when his half smile tipped the balance. "No. I'm not much of a grudge holder. Or much of a fighter, for that matter. If you really want to know, this is the first time I've ever fought with a woman."

"Ever?" she asked, not quite sure what to make of that. "Are you that easygoing?"

He swallowed and looked up to the ceiling. "Yes and no."

Then, looking back to her, he clarified. "It's true that little stuff doesn't bother me much. I mean, there are things to get upset about and things that just don't matter so much. But before you...I was never invested in a relationship like this."

"It's that different with us?"

"Yeah. So how about you, Megan—still scared?"

This time it was Megan who looked to the ceiling.

"Yes. But you're worth the risk."

Pulling her hand up so it rested on his chest, Connor played with her ring a moment, the look on his face telling her there was more on his mind. Something that perhaps wasn't so easy to say.

He frowned and his focus on her ring intensified, as though looking at it was somehow an anchor against his thoughts. Then, after a moment, he cleared his throat. "I get it, you know. What scares you about this. Us. Me.

"You don't want to end up putting your faith in a guy like your mom married—who's going to make you promises and then walk away. You don't want to *let* yourself get hurt that way again. And the fact that you're trusting me— Megan, I swear, I'm not going to let you down."

"I know," she whispered, sensing Connor's growing tension, but unsure what was driving it. "Connor, what's going on?"

He cleared his throat again and then turned to face her. Those dark eyes, achingly open to her. "I want you to know that I understand where you're coming from because I know how it feels to be left behind. To let yourself need someone and have them leave."

There was a long pause while Megan wondered if he was going to say any more. In the end she couldn't bear it any longer. "Why, Connor?"

"I think…I think I've I told you about my mother," he started.

Megan's heart began to thump. "She died when you were young."

A nod. "What I didn't tell you… What I don't tell…anyone is that she took her own life."

Megan sat up in the bed, tucking her knees beneath her as her hand flattened against Connor's heart. "Oh, Connor. I'm so, so sorry."

Patting her hand, he gave her an appreciative nod and pulled her back down against his chest. "Thank you, sweetheart. She'd been very unhappy for a long time. And eventually, it was too much for her."

"But you were only thirteen."

Her stomach knotted. Suddenly, so many pieces fell into place. Connor's bond with Jeff. His resentment toward a man who didn't deserve the title *father*. Why he understood how difficult it was for her to trust.

There were a lot of ways a person could be left. And her husband had firsthand experience with one of the worst.

"I've had a long time to come to terms with it. And like I said, I don't really talk about it. But you're putting your faith in me. Trusting me. And you deserve to know that I understand what that means."

Throat tight, she nodded against his chest. He was talking

about her trusting him, but in that moment, all Megan could see was the trust Connor had just put in her.

She was going to be worthy of it.

CHAPTER SIXTEEN

THE HOT SPRAY OF THE SHOWER blasted his face as, hands against the marble wall, Connor tried to pry his thoughts from under the duvet and the sexy little nymph he'd left buried beneath it. Five was too early to wake her with the kind of kiss on his mind. Especially since *she'd woken him* around two with a custom version of her own.

God help him, she was incredible.

Even better, *insatiable*.

And the level of compatibility between them—undiluted by vanilla vodka and unfettered by the doubts Megan had finally found her way around this past week—was off the charts. Beyond expectation.

He'd known she was smart. Had been impressed by her ability to intelligently discuss nearly any topic to come up, add her own unique perspective, find the humor in related connections. But now that she'd relaxed into the trial, she'd truly opened up... and that brain of hers *blew his mind*.

Megan made him want more than he'd imagined he could with a wife. And because of who she was—how she was—he could relax and enjoy...without worrying about leading her on.

Because his sweet, sharp, smoking-hot wife had the very same limitations he did.

Neither one of them fell in love.

Like neither one of them wanted anything more than exactly what they had.

Okay, that wasn't quite true. Connor wanted more.

He wanted this trial behind them and any lingering doubts that kept Megan from putting it there assuaged.

He wanted her pregnant.

At the idea alone, he groaned. Megan growing big and round with his baby. So damn hot.

Okay, the DNA portion of this merger and acquisition had to wait, but the rest…

Water streaming down his face, he shot a look toward the room they shared. She *had* woken him first. In his book, turnabout was fair play. His hand was already on the knob for the tap, when he remembered Megan had to work today.

Like he had to work today.

One of them at least should get more than three hours of sleep…eventually.

Wisps of cool air slipped through the steam an instant before Megan's slender arms wrapped around his waist, and her breasts, warm and hard-tipped, pillowed against his back.

"Good morning, Mr. Reed," she murmured, pausing for a decadent little lick over his spine. "Thought you could sneak out without my good-morning kiss?"

He turned, taking her in his arms so the water would reach her, as well.

She was sleep ruffled, sexy and soft. Her bare, wet skin a temptation he wondered if he'd ever be able to resist.

"Not a chance." Sinking into a slow, deep kiss, his body hardened and his mind blanked of anything beyond all the creative ways he could get her to say his name in the next hour.

Work could wait.

"One night in Las Vegas? And you knew?" came the delighted question from Georgette Houston, her bright eyes darting eagerly from Megan to Connor and back again.

Nearly six weeks into a marriage based, at least in part, on Connor's desire to have a fundraiser-ready wife on hand to balance the social against his business, and this intimate dinner squeezed in before Connor's trip to Ontario and her looming deadline was their first night out with another couple. Larry and

Georgette Houston. Both in their mid-fifties and both treating Connor and Megan more like family than a longtime business associate with a deal to pitch and his tagalong wife.

Megan opened her mouth to answer, happy to share the sanitized version of their meeting—as it had been told to her, anyway—when Connor beat her to the punch, a goofy grin hanging on his one-sided smile.

"Neither one of us was looking for romance, but we ended up talking, and talking, and talking some more. One thing led to another and…well, here we are." Connor leaned in, his arm stretched across the back of Megan's chair in the kind of comfortably possessive posture that sent butterflies skirting around her stomach. "Larry can tell you, when an opportunity as spectacular as this one presents itself, I'm not one to risk losing it. I wasn't letting Megan out of my sight until I'd secured a date for the rest of our lives."

Georgette's hand fluttered to her chest as she sighed over the romance of it all.

Larry exchanged a good-humored look with Connor, muttering something about getting the point loud and clear, and promising to have a look at the numbers Connor was sending over to him the next day.

The dinner continued for another few hours, the conversation easy and entertaining. Megan could tell Connor respected the older man and truly enjoyed his company. The laughter around their table was rich and warm, and by the end of the evening, she felt as though she had two new friends.

Friends she hoped to keep for a lifetime, because a lifetime was what she was looking at with Connor. What she wanted. What she was thanking her lucky stars for granting her the second chance to have.

Letting down her defenses had been one of the most difficult things she'd ever done. But forced to see what her fears were making of her—she'd had to try.

And once Connor had teased that trust from the tight hold of her fist…handing it over had been incredible. A heady, addictive thing. A release she'd never allowed herself to truly experience before.

And she felt…free.

Safe.

As if maybe fairy tales came in varieties she hadn't known existed. And this one was hers.

As the men collected their coats, Georgette took Megan's hands in her own, squeezing warmly.

"I can't tell you how thrilled we are Connor found you. He had such a rough start with that father of his. He's earned the happiness you two obviously share."

"Thank you, Georgette."

The older woman shook her head, a little crease forming between her eyes. "To think how close you came to missing each other."

Megan's head cocked to the side. They'd agreed not to share the part of their "love story" where she'd woken up without a memory and tried to leave, so she didn't know exactly what Georgette was referring to. "Because of the short window of opportunity in Vegas?"

The smile at Georgette's lips faltered, her gaze shifting to Connor and back. It was only the smallest slip, really, before a wide, reassuring and yet somewhat less sincere smile replaced it. "Of course."

Pulling her in for a hug, Georgette whispered, "I've never seen him look at anyone the way he looks at you. You're special."

This time it was Megan's brow furrowing, her mind churning over that instant of hesitation and the words that were setting off quiet alarms in the back of her mind. As Georgette released her, Megan opened her mouth to ask…and then stopped. She was being paranoid. *Cynical.* Looking for nonexistent problems behind words that shouldn't have been anything but the most beautiful reassurance. So instead she replied with a heartfelt truth.

"He makes me feel that way."

And then Larry was wrapping Georgette in her coat, and the

goodbyes, well-wishes and promises for another dinner were filling the space around them and the night out was at its end.

Only, one look at Connor, at that half smile she had no trouble reading at all, and she knew—for them—the night was just beginning.

Connor kicked the hotel door closed and, toeing off his shoes, dropped into the unwelcoming cushions of the couch with a groan. It was official. Megan had spoiled him completely.

He'd gotten hooked on the wind-down of their nightly conversations. On the company of a woman whose mind kept him guessing and eager for more.

And now, for the first time in as long as business travel had been a part of his life, he was keenly aware of what he was missing at home.

It sucked.

Yeah, he still got off on the negotiations, bouts of hardball and the pursuit of his goals. But here at the end of the day… something was missing.

Eyes glued to the monitor in front of her, Megan tried to focus on her last line of code. Only, something inside her balked, grinding a mental heel into the ground of her concentration.

She needed a break. Some food.

The rattle and clink of coins spilling from a slot machine— Connor's latest text tone—had her lips curving and the lethargy weighing her down evaporating into thin air.

11:37 p.m.…CONNOR: You up?

Delighted, she responded, asking how the meetings had gone. She'd missed him like crazy. No matter how much she'd told herself to rein it in, she hadn't been able to. And now—

The front bell sounded. Was he back? Here to surprise her?

She sped downstairs, hoping to find Connor waiting. Only, as she reached the first floor, her phone rang again. Answering, she swung the door open and felt her heart flip in her chest.

"Oh, my God, I love you," she gasped, blinking back tears.

The delivery guy nodded. "I get that a lot, actually."

Amused, Connor asked through the line, "You two need a moment alone, or you ready for dinner?"

Twenty minutes and half a sausage-and-mushroom thin-crust later, Megan was curled into the living room couch, phone to her ear as she watched the flames flicker in the gas fireplace.

She could hear the rustle of fabric through the phone, the weary groan—and more than anything, she wished she was there. "I'm glad you called."

"I've gotten kind of used to catching up at the end of the night. I like it."

Megan closed her eyes, snuggling into the sound of Connor's voice. "Yeah, I do too."

"So this marriage thing…it's working out for you?"

A smile played at the corner of her lips. "Yes, Connor. You've proven yourself to be quite the provider."

"That's not— Okay, good."

Megan's eyes were open wide then, something in her heart snared on the broken edge of what he'd been about to say. "It's working out for me. Like you said it would." Her voice quieted. "Even better, maybe."

A part of her expected some kind of cocky response. But instead, a long breath sounded from across the miles. "For me too."

CHAPTER SEVENTEEN

"I'M TELLING YOU, it's a done deal." Connor spun his chair away from his desk, letting his gaze run the familiar lines of downtown San Diego from his top-floor corner office.

"Yeah?" Jeff asked. "Trial's over? You guys starting production on Connor 2.0?"

He nodded. "Any day now."

Hell, probably tonight, based on the way Megan had lured him back into bed that morning. Twice.

Fortunately his first meeting hadn't been until ten, because nothing would have kept him from taking delivery of the naughty promises in his wife's eyes when he'd leaned over the bed to kiss her goodbye and she'd taken hold of his tie and tugged him down on top of her. Or after he'd showered and come back out of the bathroom to find she'd slipped into his suit shirt, buttoning only two buttons and leaving the necktie in a loose knot to trail down the seductive valley between her breasts.

Her game of dress up had cost him a good hour...and the tie, he thought with a satisfied grin.

"That's what I hear. Amazed you kept the lid on it as long as you did, but these last couple weeks—I can't go anywhere without somebody's wife bringing up your marriage."

Connor's eyes narrowed, tension winding up the base of his skull. "And?"

"And there's all the usual speculation you'd expect under the circumstances. Caro. The quick turn between. But then the people who've actually been out with you—Clausens, Stalicks,

Houstons—they're telling everyone it's the real deal. They've never seen you this way."

"Me?"

"Apparently you're in love. Everyone can see it. Brings a tear to my eye."

Pushing a short laugh past the uncomfortable knot in his throat, he deflected, "You're watching *Steel Magnolias* again, aren't you?"

"Always with the jokes."

"I'm a guy. That's how it works. Stop by after knitting club some night and I'll explain."

Jeff let out an amused snort. "Just for that, I'm learning. And someone's going to have a very special Christmas coming up."

This time it was Connor laughing, because it was entirely possible he was going to find some handcrafted atrocity in his stocking this year. "Jeff, I'm not denying there's something incredible between us. But neither Megan nor I are under the misconception it's love. Everyone else? Hell, people see what they want to and make assumptions based on what they expect. I'd rather they assume we're in love than suggest something less flattering."

"I get it. And look, I was just curious if something had changed."

"Hell, no," he clarified in no uncertain terms. "That total annihilation of boundaries isn't a game I'm into. Megan and I have a deal, and love isn't a part of it, thank God."

Even if he took his parents out of the equation, Connor had seen it too many times before with his friends, with his business associates. Love changed things. Expectations. Relationships stopped working within the framework they were established, and suddenly everything turned fluid—became a constantly changing playing field based on emotions that had come off the chain. There was no more reason. Just a vulnerability that—best case—was mutual.

"No worries, Megan and I both know the score. I made sure up front. You know I wouldn't let her get hurt." Then for a little sport, threw in, "So go find your own wife and stop worrying about mine."

"Yeah, but who says it's *your wife* I'm worried about."

Another night of champagne toasts and charitable endeavors behind them, Megan stood before the mirror in her dressing room, trying to wrestle the clasp on the sapphire necklace Connor had given her the night before. The stones, warm from her skin, winked and glittered beneath the lights, begging her to leave them on.

Her hands fell away from the clasp as Connor stepped into view behind her. His hands smoothed outward over the terrain of her shoulders, then, following the cut of the back of her dress, met again at her spine where he unhooked the top catch.

Working the zipper down the length of her back, he dropped a kiss atop one bare shoulder and then moved to the other side to do the same. "So…I was thinking about our honeymoon."

The stiff fabric of her midnight gown fell forward, gaping in the kind of provocative way Megan had never associated with herself, until now.

"What about it?" she asked, trying to concentrate on what Connor was saying, though all she seemed to register was the play of his thumbs over her newly exposed skin.

His hands slid over her waist between the loose fabric of her dress and skimmed around the front. Wide palms and strong fingers explored her hips and belly before smoothing back up to capture her breasts in his palms.

"I was thinking I ought to take you on a real one." A gentle suction pulled at the skin behind her ear as his words pulled at the tender place inside her. "You don't remember our wedding. Or our courtship…brief as it was. I want to give you a honeymoon to remember."

A memory to keep.

Hot emotion rose fast from the well she'd thought dry, pushing itself past her lips in a gasp and her eyes in a flutter of salty drops she blinked away as quickly as they came. Turning in Connor's arms, she caught his face between her palms and kissed him. Felt her dress pool to the floor as his hands molded to her bottom, pulling her close and lifting her until they aligned in all the right places.

Her legs wound at his waist as Connor carried her to the bedroom, his mouth making devilish work of the skin across her chest, along her neck and behind her ears. His tongue making promises his body would soon deliver.

How could it be like this with him? How had she ever lived without him? She pushed the questions aside, knowing she wouldn't ever have to again.

Connor wasn't going to leave her. He wasn't going to change his mind.

He'd made a commitment to her different from any of the promises she'd heard in the past. He'd shown her what kind of man he was. Made sure she understood what his word meant. She knew, with him in her life, she finally had someone to count on.

She could let go of all the defenses and anxieties with him.

She could trust him. With everything she had. For as long as they both should live.

An echo of those words whispered through her mind as her back met the soft resistance of their bed. Connor's flushed face and suspiciously disheveled hair—almost as if someone had spent a good amount of time working their fingers through it— flashed through her mind. The look in his eyes... It was like nothing she'd seen before. It was relief and awe and humor and victory and desire all there for her to see. All there, focused on her. As he said the words *For as long as we both shall live...*

Not a fantasy. Not her imagination.

Memory.

Reality.

A night she'd thought lost to her forever.

There in his eyes had been the answer to a riddle she'd struggled to solve. An answer she'd found her way to through a different path, but now... God, the way he'd looked at her. The confidence she'd felt looking back at him... It was the kind of confidence that lasted forever.

It was why she'd been able to make a decision in one night, which had taken her nearly two months to come to after.

"I don't need a honeymoon," she whispered, her fingers sifting through the silk of his hair as Connor worked down the line of her body.

"Sure you do." His tongue flicked at the hollow of her navel, briefly blanking her mind of anything beyond the wet, teasing contact. "Turks and Caicos, Tahiti, Venice, Niagara Falls?" He kissed lower, carefully catching the edge of her lacy panties between his teeth before slipping his fingers beneath and gently sweeping them down her hips and off her legs.

The playful glint in Connor's eyes was gone as he stood at the foot of the bed, staring down at her where she lay, waiting for him. She was bare of everything except the exquisite necklace at her throat and the matching slender heels at her feet.

Propped up on her elbows, she gave in to the wicked impulse to tease, sliding one knee against the other as she watched him work the buttons of his shirt with a determination she'd never witnessed before.

He'd made it to the fourth button when she straightened her leg and, using the peep front of her heel, caught the leather strap of his belt and tugged. His eyes, a dark blaze, flickered to meet hers just as she sank her teeth into the swell of her bottom lip.

For an instant, everything came to a stop. "You're a fantasy, Megan."

And then the rest of the buttons came loose in a quick series of pops as he ripped the shirt open.

Wide shoulders jerked free from between the lapels of the now-ruined shirt. The belt was gone next and then Connor was on the bed, crawling up her body even as his hand slid under her bottom and pulled her down to meet him.

Connor had to have her.

His wife didn't flaunt it for everyone to see—thank God—but she was the sexiest thing he'd ever laid eyes on.

If he'd had an ounce more patience, he would have gotten the damn pants off before he'd gotten on top of her. Only, the business with the belt and the lip biting about did him in. He needed contact. Now. Needed to feel those gorgeous heels at his back and the soft cradle of her thighs around him. He needed the wet sanctuary of her mouth and the sharp tug of her fingers in his hair.

Again he pulled her against him, rocking into the sweet spot between her legs. Torturing himself with the layers remaining between them because he couldn't make himself break away from the too-necessary contact.

Only then Megan snaked her hands in to work his fly—a look of utter concentration in her eyes as she caught the waist of his tuxedo pants and boxers with her heels and pushed them down his body.

When she'd gotten them as far as she could, he kicked them free and met her eyes. "Impressive."

The smile on her face was priceless, as if she'd accomplished the greatest feat imaginable...or the most critical task at least... by divesting him of his pants—hands-free.

The pink tip of her tongue wet her bottom lip as she held his gaze.

"I've got mad skills," she stated breathlessly.

"So you do." The smile curving his lips might have seemed out of place in the midst of this kind of sexual urgency, except fun always seemed to find a place when they were together.

Megan's eyes went to his mouth and then her fingertips drifted to the same place, feathering softly over his lips. "Beautiful."

Women had been complimenting his looks for most of his adult life, but never had such a simple statement had such a profound effect. Looking down into her eyes, he wanted to get lost in them. Wondered how he hadn't had to fight off a thousand men in Vegas to get to her himself.

And then he realized. This look he wanted to lose himself in forever... It was for him. Only for him.

He needed to be inside her. Needed it the way he needed his next breath. More, even.

Pushing to his knees, he leaned over toward the nightstand beside the bed and reached for the drawer—only to have Megan's hand follow the line of his arm and wrap around his wrist, urging him to stop.

His eyes went back to hers. "Condoms, sweetheart."

"Wait." Holding his gaze, her palm drifted down his chest, stilling over his heart. "Just you, Connor. Nothing between us." She swallowed, took a slow breath. "I don't need any more time to decide. To know."

Connor blinked. This was it.

What he'd been waiting for.

She was his. Finally.

She was...*crying*?

The hot surge of satisfaction beating its way through his veins froze as he stared at the still-shimmering smudge beneath her eye. The single glittering bead of betraying emotion caught in the dark points of her lashes. Lashes framing those gorgeous, trusting eyes that were staring up at him with—with so damn much—

"Megan," he croaked, then muttered a curse, closing his eyes when the pliant, sexy body beneath him went tense.

No. No, it wasn't love. She'd told him herself that she didn't fall in love.

Neither of them did.

What he was seeing was affection. The affection he'd been working for, cultivating from day one with the intent of securing her commitment. Only suddenly seeing it shining up at him from those trusting eyes, as his wife offered him the very thing he'd been striving for, granting him the unfettered access to her body that would cement them together forever—he recognized it for what it was.

Too much.

She wasn't supposed to look at him like that. As if she was entrusting him with a piece of her soul. Making herself vulnerable in a way he couldn't abide.

"I thought you wanted this," she said, all the breathless pleasure of only moments ago replaced with uncertainty, hurt and confusion.

"I do. You know I do...only..." Damn it, he couldn't believe he was going to say this. Couldn't believe he had to. Forcing a laugh he didn't feel, he burrowed his face against the soft shell of her ear. "You've been drinking champagne tonight... and after what happened with the wedding...I think we ought to make our most important decisions over coffee and toast."

"But—"

"Shh." Catching the slender arms that had sought to stop him scant moments ago, Connor pushed them above Megan's head and held her wrists in the loose clasp of one hand as he reached for the nightstand drawer.

A moment later, he was buried inside the tight sheath of Megan's body...working to convince them both to forget about the barriers—both physical and emotional—he'd put between them.

CHAPTER EIGHTEEN

THOUGH CONNOR HAD MADE a playground of her body, pleasuring her time and again until she didn't have the strength to do more than melt into the warmth of his body—as the minutes drifted by with the night shadows, the hours with the darkness, sleep didn't come.

She'd offered him what he'd been asking for. What he said he wanted.

She'd offered him *herself.* Their future.

And he'd turned her down.

No. It wasn't rejection. That was what she'd come to through those sleepless hours. It was protection.

Connor felt he'd failed her the night they married, and he wouldn't risk letting her make a decision as monumental as this if there was any chance her judgment might be impaired.

It wasn't rejection at all. It was a good thing.

It was further evidence of the kind of caring she was learning she could count on from the man she married.

A smile curved her lips as she heard his rapid descent down the stairs. There were definitely worse things than having a man committed to her well-being.

Checking her reflection in the microwave door, she pushed a few wayward strands of hair behind her ear, then smoothed her hands over her abdomen, desperate to calm the butterflies within.

With the coffee carafe in hand, she stepped over to the intimate nook and then poured two mugs.

A second later, Connor rounded the corner, immaculately dressed, every hair in place. He flashed her a smile and grabbed a triangle of toast from the plate she'd set.

"Perfect, I'm running late."

Before she could do more than open her mouth, he'd dropped a kiss on her cheek and thrown back half the coffee.

Taking the mug with him, he paused at the doorway, his eyes flickering to the carafe in her hand and the half-eaten toast in his.

Connor met her eyes and she saw the recognition there. The heart that had been too stunned to beat suddenly picked up, warming the chill within her chest.

"Toast and coffee," she offered with a small smile.

Connor set down his mug at the counter, his expression reserved. "Megan, you've got to believe me when I tell you how honored I am you feel like you're ready to make this commitment. And I want it. I do."

Except he didn't. She could see it in the lines of his face. Hear it in the strain of his voice. Feel it in the sinking pit within her belly.

"I don't understand." The words had passed her lips, pleading and broken before she'd had the chance to consider them. Hold them back in an effort to protect her pride. "It sounds like you're telling me no. Like—"

Like all the fear and worry she'd reasoned herself out of the night before had been more justified than she'd allowed herself to believe.

Connor crossed to her, taking her shoulders in his hands. "I want it. But the more I consider the situation, the more important I believe it is you take the full term of the trial to decide."

She searched his eyes, refusing to give in to the tears stinging her own. "You were so certain before. You didn't have a single doubt."

"For myself, I don't, Megan. But for you— Hell. I know how well you'll fit into my life. I'm not entirely sure you've had enough opportunity to see how I'll fit into yours."

She shook her head. "How can you say that? I've had two months—"

"The first one didn't count. Take two more. Be sure." He dropped a kiss on her forehead and then set her back, changing the subject as though they'd been talking about the weather. "I've got meetings late tonight and first thing tomorrow, so don't wait up. I'll probably crash at the office."

And then he was gone.

Connor's fists clenched, his knuckles turning white atop the dark mahogany of his office desk as the image of Megan's stricken face once again flooded his consciousness.

Damn it, he'd known better. But he'd been so hell-bent on convincing her to commit, to see he was the man she wanted, he'd in essence become a man he wasn't. And those tears— that overflowing well of emotion in her eyes—were all the evidence he needed to know the whole married courtship had gotten out of hand.

A quick knock sounded a moment before his secretary's head popped past his office door. "Excuse me, Connor, but the conference call with Zurich is starting in five minutes. Did you need me to send those files…?"

She'd let the words trail off rather than actually saying what they both knew. Those files he'd been working on and had promised to have to her a half hour before. Those files he still hadn't finished.

Damn it. This wasn't the guy he was.

He needed to get his head on straight. He needed to get some perspective. And he needed to make sure the man he was giving Megan was the man she'd be spending the rest of her life with.

He was confident she'd still want the marriage.

Even after a readjustment in expectations, there was no way her plan could compete with his.

But first things first. The office. That was how it had always been. How it always would be.

"Stella, see if they can push back a half hour. I'll get the files to you in twenty. My apologies for the inconvenience. Yours and theirs."

Time to get his focus back where it belonged.

The front door sounded with the muffled thud Megan had been pretending not to listen for since the previous morning. Connor had told her he wasn't coming home, but a part of her had been hoping.

Waiting.

Trying not to think of all the sleepless nights she'd spent as a little girl, weighing every creak and groan, listening for a return that wouldn't come. Because despite Connor's abrupt change of heart regarding moving forward with their marriage, she knew he was coming back.

He wasn't walking away. He wasn't leaving her.

This wasn't the same kind of blindside. Startling, yes, but not devastating.

He was looking out for her. Taking the extra time to ensure they didn't face the same doubts that had been a part of their first month together.

And now Connor was home. Back. Hanging his coat in the closet and dropping his keys on the table, offering the same greeting he did every night.

"Hello, Mrs. Reed."

Relief surged through her as she closed the distance between them, offering the kiss that had become a part of their routine from nearly the first. Everything was fine. Nothing had changed.

She wanted to bury her head in the front of Connor's shirt, press her forehead against the hollow at the center of his chest and give in to the emotion threatening to overwhelm her. She wanted his arms around her, his reassurance hot against her ear. She wanted all his sensible reason, soothing the wild insecurity that had plagued her since the minute he'd walked out the door.

Only, insecurity was a part of her she couldn't stand. It was something she didn't want in this life she was building, and so rather than collapsing against the man she'd literally been aching for, she satisfied herself with the sight of his easy smile. With smoothing the shoulder of his shirt as she asked how his day had been. If he'd slept all right at the office apartment. With his assurance that he'd been fine—had spent so many nights there it felt as much like home as this apartment.

Then ducking down into his messenger-style briefcase, he pulled out a manila folder, flashing the same smile he'd had walking in the door. The one that had her attention snared, but didn't last long enough for her to identify why.

Maybe he was tired, regardless of what he'd said about the comfort of the apartment.

"Got time to talk honeymoons?" he asked, heading past her to the living room.

A relieved laugh burst from her lungs as she followed, giddy elation bubbling up within her.

Nothing had changed.

She was the one who should have gotten more sleep.

Settling into the couch, Connor flipped open the folder and then started sorting the brochures within.

Megan tucked her feet beneath her. "So I see you have some ideas."

Only, then she saw what they were...Zurich, Munich, Taiwan.

"Not so much of a secluded-beach guy, huh?" she asked, a numbness creeping over her with the awareness of what these locales signified.

Connor shrugged, stacking the brochures in piles and then revising the order. "I like the beach fine, but what I'm thinking is it makes more sense to kill two birds with one stone."

Kill two birds...? She looked at the piles again.

"I need to get out to each of these locations for business in the next month..." Connor left the rest of the sentence to hang as his hand smoothed over her shoulder. "Hey. I know we were talking about making it some romantic-fantasy thing, but after the meetings I had yesterday and today, it's time to get my head out of the clouds and back to reality. I'm happy to take you on a trip. But practically speaking, one of these places is going to get us the most mileage. I'll get my meetings taken care of, while you take in the sights. Hit a few tours. Do some shopping."

That creeping numbness began to melt off beneath the heat of her rising temper. What in the—?

He'd been the one to suggest the honeymoon. The romantic destinations. But of course, that had been before she'd offered herself up on a platter. Megan stared back at that easy smile and indulgent expression, feeling for the first time as if the man in front of her was a stranger.

...time to get back to reality...

Was that what this was? Some kind of warning before she committed? Connor's way of making sure she understood this life ahead of them wasn't always going to be sunshine and roses?

"Hey, if you're dying for some beach time, though, you could take a trip to Hawaii. Or maybe hit a spa somewhere. Take a girlfriend with you."

She held up a staying hand. "I get it, Connor."

The honeymoon was over. And she was about to see a side of her husband he hadn't shown her before.

CHAPTER NINETEEN

DONE UP IN ANOTHER DESIGNER gown, Megan sat tucked into the back corner of the limousine, watching the lights and windows pass in a blur. Eyes shifting to the opposite seat, she noted Connor sorting through the work he'd brought along when they'd picked him up from his office a few minutes ago.

He'd greeted her with a kiss—chaste as it was—compliments on her gown and hair. A question about her day.

And yet nothing about it seemed real.

Yes, he listened to her answers, cataloging the information for later use. But the connection they'd shared from the start— that invisible something weighting every comment, every question, every small smile or subtle glance with meaning and value and *more*—had evaporated with her offer of what he'd sworn up and down he wanted.

Of course, Connor was still pleasant. Still charming. Still available to answer her questions or provide an hour or so of company at the end of the night. But the interaction was a mere shadow of what it had been in the weeks before.

Her husband had become the list of attributes he'd provided that first day they spent together.

Had this been what he'd meant their marriage to be from the start? The romance, the laughter, the intensity of the connection between them…was it all simply Connor reeling her in? Securing her affection and interest so she'd consider his proposition?

She couldn't believe it, couldn't understand why he would

have tried so hard to give her a taste of something she wasn't going to be able to keep.

Unless it was some sort of test. Connor ensuring she understood just exactly what she was committing to give up?

No, he wouldn't be so cruel. She *knew* him, and he would never intentionally do something to hurt her that way.

Besides, the kind of connection between them couldn't be faked. It wasn't something to manufacture. And it hadn't been one-sided.

So what was this?

Her eyes drifted across the car. Connor's focus was fixed on the spreadsheets in front of him. His flawless features intense. And yet nothing like the way he'd looked at her.

Was it possible he'd been as deeply affected by the unexpected connection between them as she and it was just too much…too soon? He simply hadn't had a chance to get comfortable with it and had forced a step back?

Maybe all he needed was time.

And maybe she was a self-deluding fool. But she'd told Connor once he was worth the risk, and having tasted how sweet it could be between them, she still believed that.

Yes, the idea of the man she married turning off his emotions so suddenly, so completely, was terrifying…but she couldn't accept Connor was capable of such callous indifference.

Maybe all he needed was time to adjust. Time and a little space to get his head around what was happening with his heart. And then that undeniable connection would do the rest.

She could wait. For him…for them, she would be the wife he wanted, until he realized what it was he needed. Yes. They were worth it.

Megan turned toward the window, blinking back the tears that had come with her revelation and the certain soul-deep knowledge everything was going to be fine.

Suddenly she felt so much lighter.

Moments later, the car pulled up outside the gold hotel awning. Connor set his documents aside, touching a finger to the phone at his ear. "We're at the hotel, so the rest of this is going to have to wait. You around tonight?"

His eyes flashed to hers, checking to see how she'd take the news he was scheduling a midnight meeting with one of his managers.

She offered an easy smile, then pulled a small compact from her beaded clutch and shifted her attention to a reflection she couldn't care less about. Same glossy lips and matte-finished face.

The only change was her understanding of what had happened to her marriage through the past week...and how she intended to go on from there.

Together.

She could wait for Connor. Because they were worth it.

Connor let out a short cough a long minute later. "Yeah, sorry, still here. Tonight, then. Talk to you in a few hours."

Returning the mirror to her bag, she smiled up at Connor, refusing to acknowledge the slight furrow in his brow or the way his eyes had narrowed on her.

Sensing something different, maybe?

A surge of confidence pushed through her veins at the reminder of their connection, the depth of their awareness. Everything was going to work out.

"Ready?" she asked as the door swung open and the chilly night air slipped around them.

Connor stepped from the car, leaning back in to take her hand. "Always."

She was flawless.

By now Connor should have gotten used to how smoothly Megan fit into the fabric of his life.

She'd had the entire table eating out of her hand within minutes of their arrival. Her engaging smile and seemingly limitless font of information. The authenticity he'd found so appealing, a magnet to everyone around them.

Amazing.

He'd been concerned he'd blown it, letting things get too out of hand emotionally between them—worried there might not be any coming back from that point. But after a few days of testing this more accurate representation of the life they would have together, she'd decided. Tonight in the car...he'd seen it. Acceptance.

He'd been stunned and relieved. Hell, had he been relieved. Because he didn't want to give her up. Didn't want to lose her. Now he just needed to keep his head on straight so he didn't screw this up.

A round of laughter sounded from the group where Megan stood, the musical quality of hers standing out to his ear above the rest. Threatening to pull at the place he'd called off-limits.

Slender fingers fanned wide at her neck as, head tipped back, she enjoyed whatever story Lenny was sharing with his audience.

Beautiful.

When her eyes opened again, he turned away.

He'd about exhausted the second chances he was going to get with this woman, so no more letting go and building unrealistic expectations he wouldn't be able to deliver on. Wouldn't want to deliver on.

"So it's true?"

Connor's head jerked around toward the source of that well-cultured East Coast accent. Even in accusation, the modulated delivery was as polished as if she'd been inquiring after a great-aunt's health.

Caro.

Instinct had him ready to check whether Megan could see them, but he tamped the need down.

If she happened to be looking his way, he'd attract less attention by simply exchanging a few pleasantries before moving on. Moving out.

That was what he would do.

Collect Megan and take her out of there.

She was aware of his previous engagement to Caro and knew their parting had been a recent thing.

Of course, the specifics... He'd shared them the night they

met. Intended to share them after, as well. But first, he'd been fighting so hard to win her over. And then everything had been too good to chance ruining. And this past week, he hadn't wanted to add one more thing.

There hadn't been any urgency because he hadn't expected Caro to turn up. Only, here she was, standing two feet away, peering up at him with eyes revealing nothing of her true feelings. Her smile in place—the one he'd seen every single time they'd shared space through the duration of their relationship. Smooth. Polished.

"Caro, I hadn't heard you were back in town. How have you been?"

"How have I been, Connor?" A cool voice, a pleasant smile. "Humiliated."

His gut knotted. He should have gotten in touch with her. Told her himself.

"You shouldn't feel that way," he said. Then, hoping to ease the sting, added, "Everyone knows you left me. You broke our relationship off—"

"Our *engagement*. You were going to marry me."

He nodded, a gathering tension spreading through his shoulders. Along his spine.

"Yes. You broke off our engagement," he conceded, keeping his voice as low as she'd managed to keep hers. Even so, he could feel the burn of eyes on them. Could sense the attention this few minutes' exchange had garnered. A quick scan of the area by their table showed Megan had moved.

Good.

He'd wrap this up and then get her out of there. With Caro back in town, he needed to tell Megan everything. She might not love the timing of how it had all played out, but she'd understood that first night. He had to believe she would understand now.

Caro's voice took on a sharper edge than he'd ever heard from her, assuring even more attention turning on them. "How could you do this to me?"

He met her eyes, sincere in his apology. "I never intended

for you to be hurt. We ended the relationship and you left. Went back east—"

"Because I wanted *more from you*. I wanted you to realize what we had. What you were giving up. I've been waiting—" She broke off, the emotion in her voice spilling over into her eyes.

"You said you wanted something you knew we didn't have. Something that wasn't between us. You never implied—"

"I thought you needed to figure it out on your own. That given enough time, you would realize you wanted more than an 'understanding.' I thought you would come after me."

No. It wasn't possible. Caro couldn't be standing in the middle of this ballroom with tears spilling down her cheeks. Not this woman he'd never seen with a hair out of place, who'd never raised her voice or been anything but the most polished, lovely, impenetrable piece of porcelain beauty in his presence.

He didn't want to be the cause of her pain. Had never wanted that. "Caro, when I met Megan…"

He knew how it looked. Knew he would probably never be able to make her understand.

"Did you fall in love with her?" The words snapped past her lips with a sort of biting accusation he never would have expected. But she was hurt, and the truth was he didn't know her that well. Had never wanted to look beyond the social-elite exterior she'd shown him. "No. I'm guessing not. Just another handy assembly of qualifications falling into your lap a mere thirteen days after you suggested Bali for our honeymoon, is that about it? Too convenient to pass up. An opportunity not to be missed.

"I knew you were cold, Connor. But even for you… Does she have any idea? Probably not, considering how fast you married her. I'm guessing it won't be too long, though, before she sees through the smile and charm, your attention, affection—sees how you can turn it on and off at the flick of a switch. Walk away without a backward glance. Or maybe she doesn't care. Maybe it's the pretty packaging and size of your checkbook that matters."

Connor felt the burn of anger mingling with his guilt. He knew Caroline had been hurt, and he was truly sorry for it. If the barbs she was throwing had been directed at him alone, he would have taken them. But they weren't.

"Caro," he said, lowering his voice as he leaned closer to her. "Don't do this. People are watching."

She scanned the crowd around them, straightened her spine, and then met his eyes with bitter satisfaction shining in her own. "Yes. They are."

And just like that, he knew.

Straightening away from the woman who might have been his wife, he found Megan standing stock-still at the edge of the crowd surrounding them. She appeared frozen in place. Caught midstep on her way toward him. One hand half-extended, her mouth hanging in a mockery of the gentle smile she always wore.

"Megan," he said, taking a step toward her. "Let's get our coats."

Megan's eyes followed his approach. One blink. Two.

From behind him, soothing words sounded as a number of women moved in to try to defuse the situation with Caroline— only, she wasn't through yet.

Voice rising above the din, she called, "I was going to offer your new wife the advice I wish someone had given me—not to fall in love with you. But by the look on her face, it's already too late."

Damn it! "Enough, Caro."

Megan's lips parted on an intake of breath that may have been the precursor to a response or refutation…only, then they closed with a tiny shake of her head and a helpless smile.

His hand settled at the curve of her hip, his body moving in close enough to shield her from prying eyes. "We'll talk at home."

CHAPTER TWENTY

MEGAN WALKED THROUGH to the living room, her steps clipped and graceless, her mind a riot of fragmented thoughts, confusion and unwelcome emotion.

The door closed behind her.

The lock fell and Connor's approach echoed through the marble entry.

Dropping her wrap over the back of the couch, she stared across at the wall of glass—and the black void of the Pacific beyond—wishing she were anywhere else but there.

"I know..." A muffled curse sounded as Connor's hand ran over his mouth in the reflection. "I know you weren't...prepared for that."

Megan shook her head.

No. Not even a little bit.

"I feel like a fool," she admitted, figuring one of them should offer up the whole truth.

Connor closed the distance between them, circling his arms around her belly and pulling her into the solid heat of him. "Don't. If anyone was a fool tonight, it was me and Caroline. I still can't believe— Hell, Megan, you have to understand I never expected this from her. If I had—"

"What?" she demanded, pulling free of his arms to face him. "Bothered to tell me the truth? Shared the more damning details...so I'd have a chance to be prepared if they ever came up?"

Connor's expression hardened. "I never lied to you."

"Please. Thirteen days? And what about the wanting different things. The realization you weren't right for each other. You made it sound like a loss of interest, when in fact it was the very opposite. She'd *fallen in love* with you!"

"I didn't know— Damn it, she said—"

"Forget what she said, Connor! Anyone looking at her could see how she felt. Like apparently anyone looking at me can see the way I feel. She certainly did."

His mouth snapped shut, his eyes losing the blaze of conflict altogether as his head began a slow shake of denial. "Megan. No—"

"Relax, Connor. I already know I made a mistake."

"Megan—" Connor raked a hand through his hair, grabbed a fistful of it at the base of his skull and then shook out his hands.

What could he say?

Damn it, the look on Megan's face earlier that night. She'd been trying so hard to compose herself, to keep it together, but the hurt he'd seen in her eyes... It went hand in hand with the watery emotion he'd seen the night she'd offered her commitment. It was everything he'd wanted to avoid. Everything *he'd told her to avoid.*

"What happened with Caroline was over before you and I even met."

"I heard. By thirteen days."

"Yes. Not that it should have mattered if it was thirteen hours," he retorted. "This marriage is an arrangement between like-minded parties. It's a partnership, not a love affair. I never lied to you or kept anything of importance from you."

She looked at him then, almost stunned, as if she didn't recognize him.

He didn't like it. Not at all. She knew him already, understood him. What was happening tonight didn't change anything.

"No. You didn't. I'm the one who wasn't honest."

"What the hell are you talking about?" he snapped.

"Don't worry, Connor. The only person I lied to was myself."

He should have let her go, but when she turned to walk away, he couldn't stop himself from reaching for her arm. "This doesn't change anything, Megan. All the reasons we make sense are still the same."

Her eyes went to the spot where his hand circled the bare skin of her arm. "Have you stopped to consider, Connor, that you've been so fixated on showing me all the reasons this marriage could work, you haven't really let yourself see the reasons it might not?"

"No," he said more harshly than he'd intended. Then, grasping for the understanding he knew she deserved, he tried again. "Megan, you're upset. Hurt. Embarrassed. I get it. But you're too smart to let one night dictate your future."

"You're right. I am too smart to let a single night of discomfort get in the way of something real. Of course, we're not talking about a single night, just like we aren't talking about something real. So don't even pretend we are."

Stiffening, he took a step back. "Say it."

Say it so he could start working her back from this place he wasn't going to let them go.

Her shoulders squared. "I can't be the wife you want."

Too late. "You already are."

"Then maybe it's not me at all. Maybe it's you. Maybe you aren't the husband I want."

His hand slid from her arm, all the arguments he'd been ready to throw at her suddenly abandoning him.

They were too right together. They made too much sense.

It was all this damn emotion he'd made it a point to avoid his whole life mucking everything up.

What they needed was some perspective.

"Let's not do anything rash, okay? You need some space. Why don't I get a suit and head to the office. I've got a call tonight anyway. I'll stay there. You think. And then tomorrow night we'll talk."

Megan's desolate gaze returned to his, and after a pause, she offered him a single nod.

They would be fine.

Megan was a practical woman. Realistic, Connor reassured

himself as he grabbed a suit from his closet and packed a quick bag. She needed some space to get over her hurt. And then tomorrow—damage control.

Change of plan. He couldn't afford the distance he'd been putting between them right now. So he'd close in again. Just a little. Just enough.

Bag packed, he shook out his hands and headed downstairs.

Megan was in the kitchen. He knew she wanted away from him, and yet he couldn't stop from following the sounds of the refrigerator door closing, the clink of glass against granite, the quiet gurgle of pouring wine.

Rounding the corner, he found her standing against the counter, her glass sitting untouched beside her as she waited for him.

"Do you have everything?" she asked. Polite. Detached. Exactly the kind of considerate inquiry his ideal wife would offer.

Hollow. Too damn hollow to be coming from the woman he married.

"Almost." He crossed to her in a single stride, pulling her into him and taking what was inevitably intended to be a protest for the opportunity it was.

Upturned face.

Parted lips.

The good-night kiss he couldn't leave without.

Only, Megan's lips were stiff and unyielding. She didn't pull away. It might almost have been better if she had. Instead, she'd allowed the kiss to occur, taking it with the same cool detachment offered in her words.

That wasn't how it was between them, and he might be a jerk for pressing the point tonight, but if he was going to give her the space to think, he wanted to be damn sure he'd left her with something to think about.

He brushed his lips back and forth against hers, knowing she thought to simply ride it out. Tolerate the intimacy. But rather than give up, he pulled her closer, sliding his hand up the silky expanse of her bare back to her neck. Burying his fingers in the soft strands of gold and gently coaxing her back, he deepened the kiss, licking softly into her mouth.

At her teeth, the corner of her mouth, her soft, wet tongue.

She didn't want to respond. Didn't want to give him anything. And still, he could feel the catch of her breath across his lips. The pull of her mouth against his when, on a weak moan, she surrendered.

"Megan," he groaned, holding her tight.

Her tongue rolled softly with his, her mouth drawing at him. Taking. Giving. Until all the cold space was charged with the same current that had been running between them from the very first night—until he knew, even though he was leaving, *this* would stay with her.

When he pulled back, Megan wouldn't look at him, but he could see the red flush of her cheeks.

Her hand fluttered over her lips, and she shook her head, finally meeting his eyes with the glittering rage of her own. "Have you ever stopped yourself from taking more than someone wanted to give?"

Her words shocked him. "That's not—"

But her hand flew up, cutting him off as the first damning tear slid down her cheek—and suddenly there was nothing he could say. No defense. All he could do was watch as she disappeared around the corner in a swirl of dove-gray silk—knowing that lack of will on his part was going to cost him serious ground.

She had no defense against him.

Even seeing him coming. Bracing herself against his advance. Megan hadn't stood a chance.

She'd crumbled beneath the assault of his kiss, praying he'd say something to make her feel better—to convince her things were other than they were—clinging to the very man she desperately needed to leave.

Only, Connor was exactly who she thought he was.

A man who could turn his feelings on and off with the flick of a switch.

A man who could walk away without a backward glance.

A man who could leave one woman and, in the span of a few days, move on to the next.

He was exactly the kind of man she'd sworn never to allow herself to be susceptible to again. And as if she'd been hardwired to seek out his special brand of abuse, she'd married him within hours of meeting.

The signs had all been there. Warnings left and right. Her mind flashed back to that first night out with Georgette—the awkward moment when the silence all but screamed there was more than she knew. But instead of listening to instinct—she'd actively dismissed the concern.

Because she hadn't wanted to be *cynical*. Ha!

What she hadn't wanted was to face the truth.

Disgusted, Megan slapped a layer of tape across the top of the box. Bit the cap off her marker pen and scrawled the address of her apartment in Denver at the top.

Then, stacking the box with the other two, she looked around her at the house she'd thought would be her home. She'd spent the night breaking down the life she'd begun to build there. Dividing her belongings into two categories. Her life. And her life with Connor.

It was only the belongings from the former she would keep. And of those, there was only a handful she could pack herself and still catch her flight. The rest she would coordinate with Connor once she was back in her own space.

She didn't have any fantasies about being able to leave and wash her hands of him forever.

They were married, after all.

Legally bound.

They would need to talk. But not here. Not today.

Guilt burned through her as she thought of Connor returning to find her gone.

He'd be livid. Feel betrayed.

But Connor had become too proficient at manipulating her. And as evidenced by his infuriating kiss, she was simply too weak to resist. Which meant this was the only way.

She couldn't afford to stay in a situation where her will had become a casualty of Connor's desires.

She'd built her life around doing the smart thing. Being practical. Responsible.

It was one of the things that had drawn Connor to her in the first place.

But around him, she didn't make the smart decision. She didn't do the right thing.

When it came to her husband, she threw caution to the wind and gambled on the feel-good. Telling herself she knew what she was doing…even when she had no idea.

It wasn't the life she wanted for herself. And it wasn't the life she wanted for the child she planned to have. She owed them both more.

Which was why she was leaving. Before Connor had a chance to change her mind.

Gone. Nine in the morning and already she was gone. The house quiet and still beneath the rusty sound of Connor's breath sawing in and out of his lungs.

Goddamn it.

He'd thought she would wait. Thought her conscientious core of respect and sensitivity would be enough to ensure she wouldn't leave without talking to him. Telling him to his face it was over.

At least, trying to.

But as sensitive and respectful as Megan was, beneath all that softness, she was *smart*. Too smart to give him the chance to talk her out of anything.

So she'd worked through the night. Packing only what she could take with her. Organizing the rest for his convenience.

He wanted to topple every damn piece of furniture in the place.

He couldn't freaking believe she'd actually done it.

She wasn't supposed to leave. She was supposed to calm down enough that he could talk sense to her. Remind her of the kind of life they could have together.

But instead, she'd caught some red-eye out, leaving him to find the life he'd planned for them dismantled into piles and labeled in her hand.

To hell with that.

Hands curling into fists at his sides, he stormed out of the dark office that still smelled like sunshine.

It wasn't over.

She might have left, but it wasn't as though she was out of reach. The only reason she would have gone without talking to him was that she'd been afraid he'd be able to coerce her to stay if they'd been face-to-face.

He was going to prove her right.

Go after her. Make her see reason. Make her come back. Forget about some halfhearted kiss that stopped nearly before it began. He'd seduce her. Completely. Start with his mouth and tongue. Back her against the wall because it drove her completely wild— and yeah, he wasn't above using his body to exploit the weaknesses of hers.

And once he had her mindless, breath breaking against his ear, her hands clutching at his hair, her pleas filling the space around her, he'd use that leverage—

"You can't leave me. I won't let you go..."

The echo of those decades-old words from a man he hated to the woman who hadn't been able to resist them had his steps grinding to a stop, the blood burning through his veins running cold.

He was just like him.

No matter how Connor swore he wouldn't let him be, that bastard was a part of his DNA.

How many times had his mother tried to leave his father? Tried to break things off and start a life separate from the man who would never make her properly part of his?

He thought about that morning so many years ago. The too-small, too-still shape of her curled in on herself in the middle of her bed. The knowledge, even before he reached out to try to wake her—

What would it have meant for them if his father had respected her wishes and let her start living her own life without him?

Could she have pulled herself together? Found the will to just…live?

Opening the fist he'd had clenched since he'd torn through the house and found Megan gone, he stared down at the band of diamonds in his palm.

This was the second time she'd returned it to him.

The second time he'd completely ignored what she wanted.

Raking his hands through his hair, he balled them at the back of his skull and stared out the windows at the ocean beyond.

He wasn't his father. He'd spent his life proving it to himself and anyone who dared connect the Reed name. He'd stood at the door of his father's office that last day and turned down his money. His job. His grudging recognition.

Told him he wouldn't accept any of it. The only thing he would take were the memories of how this man had ruined his mother's too-short life with his selfishness.

And those only because, try as he might, he couldn't make himself forget.

An awful pain settled deep within him. He had to let Megan go.

It would be better for them both.

Forcing his breathing to level out, he turned around and walked back to her suite of rooms.

Once this space was cleared of her things, he'd be fine. Move on, just as he always did.

Even if *always* had *never* been like this.

CHAPTER TWENTY-ONE

MEGAN HAD THOUGHT the phone call with Connor two nights earlier uncomfortable.

Yes, she'd expected they would need to talk, say the things her absence had already announced, work out the return of her belongings and discuss a divorce. And they had. But what she hadn't expected was the call to go the way it had.

So very easily. Peaceably. Politely.

Connor's casually conversational tone—

"Do you have a lawyer already or can I get one for you?"

"Sounds like the earliest the shippers can get there is Friday. Going to be okay until then?"

"You sure you don't want any of these clothes? This blue dress was dynamite on you."

—working her over in a way no amount of hostility, accusation or railing could have accomplished. It had nearly killed her to leave, but the hurt of knowing how little her departure had affected him was so much worse. He'd turned off all emotion... in a single day. Been so unaffected, the call had unfolded more like friendly chitchat than the first step in the end of a marriage.

Back at the house, he'd been ready to "talk" her out of leaving, but he'd still been in the fight at that point. Once she'd gone and the loss was confirmed...it was as if he'd simply shrugged it off. And she'd been wrecked to have all her suspicions so quickly confirmed.

But, as brutal as having her heart crushed again was, the fresh pain of it was exactly what she'd needed to alleviate her doubts about artificial insemination and her choice to forgo relationships in the future.

She would never doubt again.

So the call, as uncomfortable as it was, had been worth it.

Or so she'd thought right up until sixty seconds ago, when she'd opened the door expecting to find the shippers on her stoop, but instead faced Connor smiling that aggravating smile at her.

"Hey, gorgeous, got something these guys can prop the security door open with. Shouldn't take too long—"

"What are you doing here?" she snapped, too shocked to soften her demand.

A careless shrug. "Didn't know if you had anyone to help, and figured it would go more smoothly with a second body. You know, make sure there weren't any problems."

Throat thick with emotion she didn't want to face, emotion she needed to put aside, she shook her head. "Connor, you shouldn't have come here. I left because—"

"Call it marital privilege." His smile stayed exactly as it was, but his eyes were hard as they scanned the guys unloading one box after another from the truck. "I'm still your husband, so might as well work it while I've got it."

Marital privilege—who was he kidding?

She wanted to argue with him, tell him how much his showing up on her doorstep—when she'd left in the earliest hours of the morning to avoid seeing him again—infuriated her. But Connor wasn't stupid. He'd known exactly how much this would upset her, and he'd chosen to come regardless because Connor always did what Connor wanted.

"Anyway, I'm here," he said, reaching over her head and wrapping his hand around the security door she'd been holding on to for dear life. "So, what do you say we haul this stuff up to your apartment and get these guys out of here?"

She nodded, trying to ignore the way his casual work shirt stretched across the broad expanse of his chest, or how when he'd leaned in to take hold of the door she hadn't yet relinquished, it put him close enough for the too-good scent of his soap and skin to tease her.

Unable to resist, she drew a deep breath through her nose and held his delicious scent within her. Savoring it as she savored the memories it spurred. Memories of late nights, bare skin and pleasure that engaged her every sense.

She'd fallen so far. So fast.

Connor's free hand closed over her waist, and she looked up into those dark brown eyes. It was a mistake. She shouldn't be this close. Shouldn't have allowed herself to be snared by the one lure sure to catch her.

The hand at her waist coasted over the small of her back, shooting sparks of sensation across her skin, sparks that threatened to reignite a flame.

"Megan," Connor said, urging her closer to all his heat.

She knew she should push away. Being this close meant getting burned, but— "Watch out, sweetheart, the guys need to get by."

Her head swung around to the first mover, who was edging around her, a box marked OFFICE in his arms.

"Thanks, ma'am."

She nodded, embarrassment blazing in her cheeks as she tried to step back from Connor's hold and into the door. Only, he held her firm, until she had no choice but to meet his eyes again.

This time she kept her head.

"Let me go so I can tell him where to put everything." So she could breathe and think and stand a chance at remembering all the reasons she needed to keep her distance from this man who wreaked havoc on her judgment.

His thumb slid in the smallest caress against the base of her spine, and then his attention shifted back to the men and the truck and the return of Megan's life to what it had been before she'd met him.

What the hell was he doing there? He'd decided to let Megan go.

Had spent the entire damn day she left getting himself to a

place where that possessive part of him all about *keeping her* was tamped down enough for him to be able to call. Talk to her *without trying to talk her into anything.* Make sure she'd made it back to Denver and was okay.

He'd done it.

Worked out a few logistics regarding the return of her things and hung up patting himself on the back for finally doing the right thing.

And then he'd gone to bed and stared at the ceiling until he finally gave up and drove into work. Where he'd spent the next eighteen hours.

When the shipping crew arrived, he'd supervised the packing of Megan's belongings. Figuring once they were out of the house—the constant in-his-face reminder of what he'd wanted and what he'd lost removed—he'd be able to relax. The vise around his lungs would ease up. The persistent knot in his gut would finally loosen. But as the last box left the house, he'd found himself following behind. Checking the truck, grilling the guy in charge about how long it would take to arrive. What precautions were in place to ensure her belongings would be in the same shape when they'd arrived as when they left. If the men who'd done the loading were the same ones who would be unloading. How long he'd been working with them.

When he realized no amount of reassurance would be enough, he decided to fly out and meet the truck in Denver.

Make sure the movers delivered her things and got out of her apartment without a hitch.

Simple. No ulterior motives involved.

Yeah, sure, fantasies about getting her beneath him, on top of him, wrapped so sweet and tight and hot around him had been running through his head on a thirty-second loop. But did he have plans to act on those fantasies?

No.

At least, he hadn't until she'd peered up at him from so temptingly close. Those eyes that had been filled with ire when she saw him waiting at her door going soft and warm as he'd gotten her out of the way of the mover.

Fine. He still wouldn't act. Her looking up at him the way she did, when he knew for damn sure she didn't want anything, spoke volumes about the sway he held with her. Too much.

And the emotion in her eyes? Yeah, no stroke to his ego had ever compared...but he still didn't want a relationship with that kind of emotion. That kind of responsibility. What he wanted was Megan wanting him...but not needing him. Not vulnerable to him. Sure as hell not trying to leave him over and over again...and simply failing.

Screw that.

No. He'd make sure she was okay and then he'd be able to take off without looking back.

With the last box delivered, Connor signed the paperwork, tipped the guys and then closed Megan's door.

Her apartment felt smaller than he remembered it. But then, there were boxes stacked in the center of each of the four rooms, eating up space. She hadn't brought everything to San Diego. Not the furniture. But her keepsakes. Books. Knickknacks.

Things he'd laughed about seeing as she unpacked them, but now wondered if he'd miss having them gone.

Opening one odd-shaped box, Megan withdrew a lamp with a beaded shade, and he found himself watching intently as she returned it to the place it had previously occupied, curious about how her life fit together without him in it.

Setting the lamp on the small table beside a reading chair, she plugged the cord into the outlet and stepped back, an unreadable expression on her face.

He couldn't tell whether she was happy to see it returned or not.

She turned to him, and he knew what was coming next. Wasn't ready for it and so cut her off before she could say goodbye.

"Which room do you want to start with?" he asked, jamming his hands deep into his jeans pockets so she wouldn't see his fists, and plastering an easy smile on his face.

"Connor, thank you for getting my things returned so quickly, but I can handle the rest."

"I'm here," he said, aware his voice had lowered. Taken a stern tone. "I'll help. Let the office know I'll be out a day or two—"

"What?" she gasped.

"We'll order some pizza, pick up a bottle of wine for tonight. Throw in a movie." He'd make it casual. Not intimidating. No demands. No pressure. Not really.

"A pizza? Are you out of your mind or are you intentionally being cruel?" She was vibrating with tension now, and suddenly Connor was right there with her.

"I'm trying to help. I want—"

"It's not about what you want, Connor! How can you not get this? I can't be friends with you!"

And then he was in her face, his hands wrapped tight around her upper arms, as he bellowed back, "I don't want to be goddamn friends, Megan!"

She blinked, as shocked by the break in his reserve as he was.

"What do you want?" she asked too quietly for the way they were locked together.

Seconds passed and then finally the breath he'd been fighting to contain shot past his throat with the only answer he had.

"I want you. I want what we were supposed to have. I want the wife and the partner I found in Vegas. I want you to admit I can give you more than you can have alone."

"It won't work."

"Why not?"

"Because—" she held up her hands helplessly, too much pain and emotion shining in her eyes to be anything other than what came next "—I love you, Connor."

It wasn't a surprise after what she'd said before moving out, or at least it shouldn't have been. He'd seen the evidence in her eyes. In her hurt. In a million little things he'd given up trying to deny. But hearing the actual words on those lips he couldn't get enough of—they hit him like a sucker punch, knocking the wind from him and leaving him stunned.

Megan walked to her door and held it open, her eyes on the floor ahead of her feet. "Please, just go."

CHAPTER TWENTY-TWO

MEGAN BACKED UP her files and then stared at her monitor. Too many sleepless nights and the desperate need to distract herself had the latest phase of her project complete well ahead of schedule.

What was she going to do now to stave off those unwelcome thoughts? The insidious whispers slipping too fast through her mind?

...good morning, Mrs. Reed... I'll take my kiss now...

Some days she gave in to them, losing herself in the memories. The pleasure she'd found in those moments. Other days, like today, she fought against them, not wanting the pain that came with the understanding of what she'd lost.

The monitor blurred.

More tears. How long would it take before she cried the last? At the sharp ache in her heart, she wondered if it would be ever.

The trill of her phone sounded. And, closing her eyes to wipe the last of her tears from evidence, she reached for the handset, welcoming whatever distraction waited on the other end.

Maybe a credit offer?

A survey?

Whoever the poor sucker was on the other end of the line, they were going to be earning their check today. She'd keep them busy for the next hour and a half at least.

"Megan Scott," she answered, still having to force it past her lips.

A pause, and she assumed it was some automated system

registering the pickup and kicking her over to a live person. Only, then—"Scott? I realize it's been a while since we spoke, but I'd have thought someone would have notified me if I'd gotten divorced."

Connor.

How was it possible for a person's heart to leap and fall all at once?

"It may not be official yet, but it will be."

"Right. Sure." He cleared his throat. "So I was over in New York a few days, but I'd been meaning to check in once you'd had a chance to get your things unpacked. Make sure there wasn't any damage. You got everything?"

A reasonable inquiry. Connor took his responsibilities and commitments seriously. That was all this was. Taking a steadying breath, she answered equally reasonably, "Everything was in perfect order. Thank you again for your help."

"Glad to hear it. You'll let me know if you realize anything is missing."

"I don't think there is."

"Terrific. So now that you're settled back in, what are your plans?"

Megan stared at the phone a moment. How could he ask? "Connor, you know what my plans are. After everything that's happened…nothing's changed." Nothing except her heart was broken into a thousand pieces and every time she heard Connor's voice, so casual and inquiring, it broke into a thousand more. "I—I really need you to let me go. I think it's better if our lawyers handle the communication from here."

You know what my plans are…

The words pounded through Connor's skull as relentlessly as a jackhammer, over and over again, until now, hours after Megan had ended the call, he felt the reverberation of them through every cell in his body.

He'd known from the start Megan had a path laid out for her future. A family without the complications of a marriage or a man. And he'd been fine with it. Because he believed it would never come to pass.

He was supposed to have time. Time to win her back. Time to figure a work-around Megan wouldn't be able to resist.

She'd fallen in love with him. Which meant she was capable of the one thing that, previously lacking, had led her to consider artificial insemination.

She'd fallen in love with him. So she was supposed to believe it would happen with someone else. Eventually. And wait.

Only now she was going to go through with it.

Nothing's changed...

Uh-huh. Not one damn thing. Except he was physically sick to his stomach thinking about Megan with another man's child. Thinking about that unbreakable connection, that intimacy of union—even if the donor never knew she existed, the idea alone was enough to put him into a near rage.

And what about all the months to come? Her relationship with her mom was tenuous at best. Who was going to be there to help her through the tough times? The times when she was sick, weak, hungry...or scared.

Hell. He hated that almost more than he hated the idea of some piece of another man mingling with the very essence of who she was.

His mother hadn't talked a lot about what it was like raising him on her own. She hadn't wanted him to feel like a burden. But he could remember a night when she'd been crying, talking to his father. Asking him if he'd any idea what it was like for her—waking up in labor by herself. Not understanding what was happening. Having to get to the hospital and spend all those hours waiting for a man who had made promise after promise, but never came to her. A man who let her deliver his child, scared and alone, while he'd hosted a Christmas party with his wife.

Megan wouldn't even have the hope someone might come.

Damn it, why couldn't she just let him be with her?

Pushing out of his chair, he walked over to the bar and poured a glass of scotch, threw it back in the hopes the burn would dull the gut-wrenching ache with all the what-ifs and why-couldn'ts constantly swirling around Megan's name in his belly.

It didn't help. So he poured another, figuring if he couldn't kill the pain in his gut, maybe he'd at least be able to numb the pounding in his head.

An hour later, he was thinking more clearly than he ever had before. Pushing the empty bottle aside, he reached for his phone.

"I need you…"

Connor woke with what felt like the better half of a landfill in his eyes and the near certainty that somehow through the course of the night he'd ended up on a cruise—the gentle rock and loll of the space around him doing things he didn't entirely love to his stomach. Only, then the mattress beneath him sagged with a shift of weight that wasn't his own.

Not. Alone.

Elation ripped through him as he tried to pry his eyelids open, experienced a stab of pain at the intrusion of light and clamped them closed again.

It didn't matter.

If he wasn't alone, then somehow, someway, he'd gotten Megan back into his bed. God bless whatever he'd been drinking last night.

Blindly reaching across the sheets, he encircled the first warmth he encountered and pulled it close. Or tried to, except—

"I don't know what you heard," said the octaves-too-low voice from considerably too close, "but I'm not that kind of girl."

Jeff.

This time Connor wrenched his eyes open, forcing them to withstand the searing pain of daylight and the utterly confusing sight of his hand wrapped around Jeff's jeans-clad thigh, where it rested atop the comforter on his bed.

His bed.

Not a cruise ship.

So what was with the sudden, violent pitch— Oh, hell!

"Yep. Bucket's right over the side, champ," Jeff stated, using his leg to shove him in the opposite direction. "Knock yourself out."

Thirty minutes later, Connor was showered and dressed. Minty freshness doing its best to disguise the funky aftermath of a night misspent.

What had he been thinking?

Dragging himself into the kitchen, Connor dropped into a chair at the table and hazarded a glance at Jeff, who was cooking steak and eggs, a smug smile on his smug face.

"Not to suggest I wasn't thrilled to find you in my bed this morning, but what are you doing here?"

A smug flip of the spatula. Damn him.

"My phone's on the table. There's a voice mail that gets the ball rolling, but I think the texts cover the gist of it pretty well. See for yourself."

The churning mess that was his stomach solidified into a lead ball. Oh, hell. Thumbing through the messages, the lead ball grew with each exchange.

8:42 p.m....REED: Need you to go to Denver w me.
8:46 p.m....JEFF: In meeting. Give me 1 hr.
8:53 p.m....REED: No can do. Want wife back. Going now. Think I cn talk her into it wth sperm.

Hell. Please don't let him have called her.

8:53 p.m....JEFF: R U drinking?
8:55 p.m....REED: Have wht she wants. Solllid plan. Better than hers.
8:56 p.m....JEFF: Leaving now. Wait 4 me.
9:02 p.m....REED: Don't worry botu it.
9:02 p.m....JEFF: WAIT 4 ME
9:04 p.m....JEFF: PICK UP YOUR PHONE
9:57 p.m....JEFF: You should stop for drink @ that bar in terminal with the big olives B4 flight
10:22 p.m....REED: Hey, UR at the bar. You look pissed.

Connor looked up at his friend. His very best friend in the entire world. "How did you do it?"

"Luck mostly. And some cash. Called your car service and got a guy ready to block your driveway—just in case. I know you don't drink and drive, but, well, you weren't exactly yourself. When you called for a ride, he was already there. Drove you to the airport, the very long way. Meanwhile, I took the chopper down and picked you up at the bar."

"And you stayed with me…in my bed…to make sure I didn't drown in my own puke?" Pushing a hand through his hair, he shook his head. This was a low like he'd never expected to see.

"Yeah, but mostly to keep you from calling Megan, dumbass. By the way, your phone met with a bit of bad luck when a meat tenderizer fell on it last night. Sorry."

Jeff slid a plate of steak and eggs in front of him and dropped into Megan's chair at the table, diving into a plate of his own. "So what's the deal?" he asked around a bite of eggs.

Nothing's changed…

"She's planning to get pregnant."

"Ah, and you thought you'd help her out. Right. Only, I'm wondering, if she didn't want you to get her pregnant before, then where did you think your swimmers were going to get you last night?"

"If I had to guess, I probably figured I could talk her into reconsidering. Make her see what I could offer her. What she was giving up."

"And that would be the material comforts. Financial security?"

Connor grunted. "At least someone sees it."

"Yeah, I see something. But I'm not sure it's the *same thing* as you."

He wasn't in the mood to decipher hidden meaning or subtle subtexts. "Spit it out."

Jeff shook his head, the lines between his brows drawing together. "Ask yourself this, Connor—what is it that's got your *man*ties in such a twist? I mean, really…what is it about Megan you don't want to lose?"

Connor opened his mouth to answer, ready to explain about how right they were together. How easy it was. Only, suddenly, he could see the past few months with a clarity he'd never had before, and a tension, different than the one he'd already become so intimate with, slid down his spine.

Their marriage had been a train wreck from about the word go.

His bride so soused she woke up the next morning unable to remember his name, let alone why she'd agreed to marry him.

She'd been a hassle from the start. The kind of work he never invested in relationships. She'd taken time. She'd taken romancing. She'd kept him on his toes, kept him working, kept him guessing. She'd infuriated and confused him.

And he'd relished every minute of it.

It didn't make sense.

In retrospect, Megan had basically brought every complication and frustration indicative of the love relationships he claimed to loathe to the table, and had him all but begging her to give him more.

She affected him like no one he'd ever met. And even knowing what kind of chaos she'd delivered upon his life…the idea of not having her in it was killing him.

Staring back at Jeff's smug, smug face, he nodded. "Okay. I think I've got it."

CHAPTER TWENTY-THREE

SIX HOURS LATER, Connor tore down the stairs, patting his pockets as he went.

Wallet? Check.

Keys? Check.

Ring box? Burning a hole in his jacket pocket. Check.

A rushed glance at his watch and his adrenaline spiked. He could do this.

The flight left in forty minutes and he'd be on that plane even if it meant buying the damn airline to ensure it. And once he got to Denver— His stomach took a dive as a thousand scenarios flooded his mind...only one of which would bring about the happily-ever-after he'd only hours before come to terms with wanting.

Shoving all outcomes but that one from his mind, he grasped the knob from the front door and—

Ticket! He hadn't printed the damn thing out, and after his phone's tragic demise, he needed the paper.

Internet station in the kitchen!

Sprinting down the hall, he almost bit it skidding around the corner.

He needed to get there.

Needed to be with his wife.

Needed to tell her it could work between them. And not because of the reasons he'd been laying on her from the start, but because of all the reasons he'd figured out once she left. All the things he realized he couldn't bear to live without.

Flipping open the computer, the black screen flashed to life, bringing up a background with a picture of the two of them at a charity dinner from the month before.

They were laughing. His fingers playing with a bit of her hair as they stared into each other's eyes.

And the way he was looking at her…how the hell had he missed it?

He'd have to wait for the plane to figure it out. There wasn't time now.

Bringing up the browser, he distractedly noted Megan's email was still open from the last time she'd used the machine. About to open a new tab for the airline, he paused as one of the bold-faced messages caught his eye and the preview shattered his plans.

It was from the sperm bank, dated five days prior.

Subject: Per your inquiry, Donor #43409089RS1 available for immediate pickup.

Megan had brought this on herself.

Blinking down at her tablet, perched on the pass-through counter dividing her kitchen and living room, she sat, a silent observer to the video chat that was Gail, Jodie and Tina's rally of support.

"Oh, and you're really surprised he got away?"

What had she been thinking?

"Shut it. You saw the way he looked at her during the re-ception."

"Shut it? Nice talk, Tina."

Well, she'd been hoping a triple dose of misery in the form of this fingernails-down-a-blackboard bickering might distract her from the misery that had begun in her heart and then slowly, steadily spread until it had overtaken every part of her being.

No such luck.

Where was a white-chocolate martini when she needed one? A white-chocolate martini of birdbath proportions with a garden hose–size Crazy Straw to expedite consumption.

"Are you joking?" Tina leaned around Gail to scowl at Jodie.

Not that she'd be able to drink it, even if one materialized out of thin air. The thought alone had her belly kicking up rebellion enough she had to close her eyes and draw several deep breaths through her nose.

Besides, God only knew what kind of mess she'd wake up in if she followed the cocktail path to avoidance again. A mess of sheets and covers…and Connor's legs tangled with her own?

No.

She wasn't supposed to want that. Had to stop wanting that. Or at the very least, stop fantasizing about ways in which to make it happen.

"You want nice talk? How about—"

"Girls," Gail cut in. *"This is about Megan. Her life is beyond tatters. Again. Another failed relationship. This time a marriage. Granted, we all know about the hasty courtship and may have had our own theories about the probability of success—"*

Jodie gasped, hand flying up to not quite cover the smile riding her lips. *"Gail!"*

But Megan's cousin simply ducked her head a pinch, holding out her hands as if to say, *We were all thinking it.*

At which point the three began a rapid-fire exchange rife with theories, speculations, the more pathetic bullet points from Megan's romantic past, a tangent about Jodie buying a pair of shoes out from under Tina, something about a sweater in high school…a boy from middle school…the Laura Ingalls Wilder books from first grade…

She might have cut them off, but the sad truth was she simply didn't care. That instant of weakness with the forbidden fantasies had opened the door to something worse—something far more devastating.

Memories. Broken bits and pieces of what had actually been. Connor…*I love it when you get my name right… I've got you. What I want is to keep you… Everything, Megan… So this marriage thing…it's working out for you? You're a fantasy… I don't want to be goddamn friends…*

Oh, it hurt so bad.

"Great, Jodie. See what you did—she's crying—"

"Me?"

"Oh, no, Megan, honey, don't cry. So maybe the whole love thing isn't for you. So what? Think about something happy."

"Yes! Think about your little sperm-bank baby!"

Megan shook her head and wiped her thumbs beneath her eyes, hating her apparent inability to keep the tears at bay.

"I'm fine. I'll be fine." Someday. Maybe. "I just need a drink."

Pushing up from the stool where she'd been seated, she circled around to the sink and poured a glass of water. Thought of the way Connor had so often shown up in her office with a cold drink or some healthy snack. The way he'd been so thoughtful and attentive to her, most of all when she'd managed to forget to be attentive to herself.

He'd been aware of her on a level no one ever had before.

But it hadn't been love.

How ironic that her inability to fall in love had been the destruction of every other relationship she'd had. And actually finding it, the destruction with Connor.

Why now?

Why couldn't she have been the wife he needed her to be?

Three swift knocks sounded at her door, thankfully drawing her out of that downward spiral of self-destructive thought.

Her eyes swung to the door, her heart tripping in her chest until she realized the security door hadn't buzzed. Mrs. Gandle from 2C had probably signed for another package.

Chastising herself for that stupid surge of hope, she walked to the door and swung it open—

"Connor?" she choked out, shaking her head in disbelief at the scowling man standing at her door, a plastic shopping bag hanging from one hand.

"No security chain?" he demanded, his outrage potent and possessive. "First some little old lady downstairs holds the door open for me, letting me march right in, and then you open the door without even checking who's out here? Megan, this is a decent neighborhood, but what the hell?"

She shook her head, too stunned to register anything beyond the fact that Connor was here.

He'd come back.

Again.

Connor shoved his free hand through his hair, acutely aware of the ass he was making of himself and yet unable to walk away as he should.

"What are you doing here?" she asked, her words barely a whisper.

He opened his mouth to answer, but then all he could do was stare. Soaking in the sight of her smattering of freckles and gorgeous mouth he hadn't seen smile for too damn long.

Her face seemed thinner and he didn't like the shadows beneath her eyes, and yet no one had ever been so beautiful as she was right then.

Clearing his throat, he looked down into the eyes that had been haunting him for weeks, and then to the hand that had come to rest defensively across her belly.

"Why did I wait so long?" he asked himself, keenly aware of the futility of the question.

Megan blinked, confusion and hurt and a thousand other things shining too bright in those beautiful eyes. And then resolve. "You need to stop this, Connor. What you're doing, calling, showing up. It's—" she swallowed, looking as though even that simple act took monumental effort "—it's hurting me."

He hated knowing it was the truth. Wishing he'd been smart enough from the start to make it so neither one of them would have had to go through this kind of pain. "I'm sorry."

"Then leave," she whispered. A single fat tear spilled over her bottom lid, and his heart twisted with a pain he'd never experienced before. "Please. I can't be what you wanted me to be. I'll never be able to be that for you. Let me go."

"No." He shook his head solemnly. "I tried. I did. But I can't."

"You have to—"

"I'll *never* let you go!" The words had ripped past his throat before he'd had the thought to temper them. But they were the truth.

Megan froze in her spot, her gorgeous mouth parted in mid-protest, brows pulled high together in an expression that was pure, helpless disbelief.

But not elation. Not blissful surrender.

At the first blink, the sign she was breaking out of that stunned state of suspension, he panicked. He hadn't said enough, hadn't explained, couldn't risk her response before he told her everything she needed to know.

So he pulled the lowest trick he had in his arsenal. This was too important to him—*she* was too important to him—to risk playing by the rules. And for the first time in his life, he didn't damn his father for that bit of unscrupulous DNA spiraling through the darkest parts of who he was.

He embraced it.

Stepping forward, he caught Megan with one hand beneath the fall of her hair, silencing any denial she might have made with a kiss bursting with every bit of aching, unfulfilled long-ing, heartbreak, desire and need he'd suffered since the mo-ment she left. He told her with his lips how he missed her, with his tongue the way of his want. Gentle bites hinted at the hold she had on him.

And when her fingers were wrapped in his shirt, her breath rushing across his lips and cheeks, her eyes again locked with his—he went on. Telling her what he'd only discovered for himself.

"Megan, I never wanted love. I saw what it did to my mother and didn't want any part of it. All my adult life I avoided that kind of intimacy, holding myself at arm's length and making unbreachable boundaries a part of every relationship. It was easy. Until I met you. In the span of a few hours, I'd married you and all the rules I lived by were a thing of the past. I swore up and down we'd have the kind of controlled marriage where no one could get hurt, but I couldn't even control myself. Noth-ing halfway was enough with you. I made every excuse in the book, but I couldn't admit what was really going on."

"Connor…" His name passed her lips on a breath that barely dared to take voice.

"I said I didn't want to be your friend, but it's not true. I want to be your friend and your lover and your husband and the father to your children—" He broke off, swallowing past a well of regret without limit. "I know you're going to tell me it's too late, but Megan, it's not."

He dropped to one knee. Watching her eyes go wide, he held up the gallon of organic whole milk in one hand and, pulling the box from his pocket with the other, flipped open the lid, revealing the two rings nestled together within black velvet. One the diamond-encrusted wedding band she'd returned to him twice already but he couldn't accept she didn't want. The other a solitaire as weighty as the promise it conveyed. "I will love this baby like it's my own. It will never know a single minute of doubt because I swear to love it as much as I love you."

Megan's breath sucked in at his confession. His revelation. His freedom.

"You don't remember my first proposal, but I'm hoping this one will stick. Megan, I love you. And I'm asking you to let me give you a lifetime of what you've shown me matters most. Laughter, love, late-night conversations. I'm asking you to be my wife in the most conventional, traditional and time-tested meaning of the word, for as long as we both shall live."

Heart slamming, breath held, he waited as his world hung in the balance.

CHAPTER TWENTY-FOUR

THIS COULDN'T BE HAPPENING. It wasn't real. It wasn't possible.

This was a nervous breakdown in action. It had to be. Something she should have seen coming...except the gallon of milk was the sort of surreal her brain typically didn't conjure.

Which meant... "Oh, my God."

Her breath left on a quiet sob and she reached for him, pulling at his shirt until he stood. Taking the milk from him, she set it on the secretary table with a small shake of her head.

"I'm not pregnant, Connor."

He stared into her eyes a long moment, the muscles of his throat working as though he was trying to make words that wouldn't come. And then he pulled her into his arms, his big body wrapping around her as ragged breath sounded against the top of her head.

Relief, powerful enough to overwhelm a man as strong as Connor, washed over her. It was humbling to witness.

"Your email was still open on the kitchen laptop," he said, his words glass-and-gravel rough. "I saw the message about a requested donor being ready for pickup."

Megan flattened her hand against his chest, the only reassurance she could offer within the decadent confines of Connor's hold. "That message was in response to an inquiry I'd made months ago. Before we met. I wasn't ready to move forward with those plans."

They were still married, for one. And the way she felt about Connor... She couldn't begin something so important with her heart still torn to shreds. She'd assumed her plans would be on hold for at least another year or two.

Releasing his python grip on her, Connor gently cupped her jaw as he tipped her face to his.

"I don't care." The steady calm of his words in direct contrast to the burning intensity in his eyes.

Her brow lifted in question.

"I want you anyway. Even if I don't get a baby in the bargain."

A soft laugh pushed past her lips. How did he do it? Make her laugh when her world was up in the air?

"You want me anyway?"

A nod. "I love you, Megan. I didn't think it was something I had in me, but that was because I'd never experienced it before I met you."

He loved her.

Connor searched her eyes, one corner of his mouth curling into a wolfish smile as the hands at her jaw slipped into her hair. Gently he urged her head back and lowered his mouth for a soft, sinking kiss that tasted like every promise she'd never allowed herself to dream of asking for. Then, fitting his lips more firmly over hers, he slid his tongue past her teeth to stroke against her tongue, once, twice, again and again, until her hands were locked in the fabric of his shirt and she was clinging to him with everything she had.

Never breaking the kiss, his hands began a slow roam over the contours of her body, following the curve of her waist and the lines of her arms. Threading through her fingers and making the world around her spin, until she was grounded by the unyielding resistance of the door to her apartment at her back. The seductive press of her wrists against the solid panels, and the mind-jumbling weight of Connor's body in full delicious contact with her own.

"I love you," he whispered against her lips.

"Oh, my God, yes."

Both of them froze at the punctured illusion they were the only two people on the planet. In the room.

"Shhhh!"

Connor's chin pulled back as he looked down into her rapidly heating face.

"I'm sorry—I forgot." How could she have forgotten?

Together they turned toward the source of the invasive words, to where her abandoned tablet sat on the pass-through counter, three eager-eyed, utterly shameless faces filling the screen.

Connor straightened, pushing back from her to walk to the electronic device. "Sorry, girls, show's over."

"No, wait!"

"Heya, Connor, nice moves."

"Dang it, Jodie! See what you di—"

Flipping the cover closed, he severed the connection and turned to face her.

She shouldn't have laughed. Really.

"Funny, is it?" he asked, a smile on his face.

"Accident," she swore, holding her hands up. "I was distracted."

"So it would seem," Connor replied, nodding toward her still-raised left hand.

Her gaze followed his to the fourth finger of her left hand, where her wedding ring glinted beside the new ring that had been nestled in black velvet when she'd last seen it.

"Sneaky," she whispered, barely able to push the word past the well of emotion at seeing her wedding band returned to her hand.

"I was hoping seeing them on your finger might help me get the answer I'm waiting for."

"I love you, Connor. And I want everything you're offering. I want to be your wife and the mother to your children. But—"

He stepped forward, all that cocky confidence falling away. "But?"

She smoothed her hand over the stubble-rough edge of his jaw before letting it drift to the buttons of his shirt. "But what would you say about waiting on the baby. Maybe taking a few months or a year—"

"A trial?" he asked, nodding quickly. Determination and

resolve pushing past the disappointment and hurt that flashed across his face. "Anything to make you feel safe. Confident."

Slipping the first button free, she shook her head. "No. I don't need any trial."

He searched her eyes. "Then what?"

"Maybe for a while, all I want is you."

"Yeah?"

Working the next button free, she nodded. "After all, we've got the rest of our lives together. Now, Mr. Reed, I'm ready for my I-love-you kiss."

That half smile pushed hard at Connor's gorgeous lips until it spread, encompassing his whole mouth and then his face.

"Gladly, Mrs. Reed," he answered, emotion making his voice gruff as he took her in his arms and dipped her back. "I love you."

And then he gave her a kiss that was meant to be the first of its kind, but tasted so familiar there was no denying those undercurrents of love had been there all the time...just waiting to be recognized. This one, though, her husband delivered wholly. Without reservation. Without limit.

It was a promise of forever...and she believed.

* * * * *

ROMANCE

MEDICAL

Mills & Boon® Large Print

April 2013

ROMANCE

HISTORICAL

MEDICAL

Mills & Boon® Hardback

May 2013

ROMANCE

A Rich Man's Whim	Lynne Graham
A Price Worth Paying?	Trish Morey
A Touch of Notoriety	Carole Mortimer
The Secret Casella Baby	Cathy Williams
Maid for Montero	Kim Lawrence
Captive in his Castle	Chantelle Shaw
Heir to a Dark Inheritance	Maisey Yates
A Legacy of Secrets	Carol Marinelli
Her Deal with the Devil	Nicola Marsh
One More Sleepless Night	Lucy King
A Father for Her Triplets	Susan Meier
The Matchmaker's Happy Ending	Shirley Jump
Second Chance with the Rebel	Cara Colter
First Comes Baby...	Michelle Douglas
Anything but Vanilla...	Liz Fielding
It was Only a Kiss	Joss Wood
Return of the Rebel Doctor	Joanna Neil
One Baby Step at a Time	Meredith Webber

MEDICAL

NYC Angels: Flirting with Danger	Tina Beckett
NYC Angels: Tempting Nurse Scarlet	Wendy S. Marcus
One Life Changing Moment	Lucy Clark
P.S. You're a Daddy!	Dianne Drake

Mills & Boon® Large Print

May 2013

ROMANCE

HISTORICAL

MEDICAL

Discover Pure Reading Pleasure with

Visit the Mills & Boon website for all the latest in romance

Buy all the latest releases, backlist and eBooks

Find out more about our authors and their books

Join our community and chat to authors and other readers

Free online reads from your favourite authors

Win with our fantastic online competitions

Sign up for our free monthly eNewsletter

Tell us what you think by signing up to our reader panel

Rate and review books with our star system

www.millsandboon.co.uk

 Follow us at twitter.com/millsandboonuk

 Become a fan at facebook.com/romancehq